Psychic Detective Files

Judith Ann McDowell

This is a work of fiction. Names, characters, places, and incidents are products of the author's imagination or are used fictitiously and are not to be construed as real. Any resemblance to actual events, locations, organizations, or persons, living or dead, is entirely coincidental.

World Castle Publishing, LLC
Pensacola, Florida

Hardback ISBN: 9798250520713
Paperback ISBN: 9798891265400
eBook ISBN: 9798891265417
First Edition World Castle Publishing, LLC, March 16, 2026
http://www.worldcastlepublishing.com

Cover: Cover Designs by Karen
Editor: Karen Fuller

CHAPTER ONE

Pat Lancaster sits quietly, going over the police files she has helped as a psychic to solve.

"Guess I have no reason to feel bad as a psychic since there are over 300 solved cases here," she murmurs aloud.

She looks up as Lieutenant Phil Abbot walks into the room to sit in the chair beside her.

"I agree with what you said. I don't know what we would do without your involvement in many of our cases."

"Thank you for your kind words, Phil. As always, you are in my corner."

"I want to talk with you about something I feel is important."

"Let's hear it," she says, smiling over at

him.

"I think you do better in getting to the root of the problems in many of these cases when DK is along to make you feel safe. Am I wrong in thinking this?"

Pat laughs. "No. In fact, you are spot on. DK and I have a strong and trusting relationship."

"I am glad to hear this. I'm also happy you aren't trying to talk the other one into quitting the police force or earning a living helping solve cases."

"We both figured out that was a lost cause. So, what is it you want to say?"

"How would you feel about DK getting off the police force and earning a living by being with you when you come in to work on solving a case for us?"

"I know we touched on this before, but we haven't gotten into it. I will have to see how DK feels about this. I think he will welcome the idea.

"Okay. Let me know what DK thinks of the idea," he says, getting to his feet as the phone on his desk rings.

"Lieutenant Abbott. How can I help you?" he listens to what is being said on the other line, then hands Pat the phone.

"Hello. Yes, this is Pat Lancaster."

Abbott stands by, waiting to see what new case is coming their way, then reaches out to take the phone Pat is holding out to him.

"I don't think this will amount to much, but the woman on the phone is distraught and wants to know what is happening. I will leave it up to you what you think."

"Okay, fill me in on what's going on."

She says she and her husband gave a beautiful lamp they purchased at an antique shop to their son for Christmas. For some reason, the light goes off and on by itself."

"Probably has a short. If she is upset, tell her to return the lamp to where she bought it and request her money back."

"I was thinking a short, too. But she is pretty upset. I'll go over to her house and check it out just to be sure."

"Are you going to take DK with you? He can probably fix the short, and she can stop worrying."

"I'll see if he is off and can go."

"Let me know. I'll get relieved of duty if he wants to go," he says, handing her a small piece of paper.

Pat pulls the car into the driveway, glad to see Dk's Rambler already there.

As she enters the house, she is met by two frisky fur babies vying for her attention with wagging tails.

"There's my baby," DK says, holding out his arms.

Pat puts both hands on the sides of his face and, pulling his face forward, plants a kiss on his parted lips.

"So good to see you home early."

"Are you working later? If you are, Phil can get you off so you can accompany me on another case."

"No. I'm off. What is the case you have this time?"

"A woman called in saying she has a lamp that goes off and on by itself. Phil and I said it is most likely a short in the lamp. He also said you can probably fix the lamp and end her thinking she has a haunted lamp in her house."

"I can give it a try. When are we going to visit her?"

"May as well go later today. First, though, I want a cup of coffee and a sandwich."

"I'll pour us both some coffee and make us a sandwich. Aren't you glad you have me to wait on you hand and foot?" He grins as he pulls a cup from the cupboard.

"Yes, I am. Right now, I want to enjoy some doggy kisses."

While Pat enjoys the attention of the two pups, DK takes the necessary meat, cheese, and different spreads from the refrigerator.

"Phil asked me about something today that may include you."

"Oh, this should be interesting."

"Since we can both accept what we do for a living, he wants to know if you would consider leaving the police force and accompanying me on my different cases. I told him I do feel more protected with you along."

DK set their coffee and sandwiches on the table and then sat back in his chair.

"Did he mention if he plans to pay me to quit my job and accompany you? We aren't millionaires."

"I am sure he plans to compensate you for your time. Just as he does me, the lady I spoke with said she would pay me a hundred dollars to help her."

Pat dabbed at her lips, wiping away the mayonnaise clinging to the corners of her full mouth.

"That is a pretty good amount to fix a short in a lamp. So, yeah, consider me hired."

"I'll tell him your decision after we return from checking out the lamp scare."

***

Pat pulls up in front of a three-story white house and turns off the ignition.

"Nice looking house. It looks like it was built a good many years ago. You know, when they cared about their work?"

Pat smiled before getting out of the car.

A woman who looked to be in her late sixties, wearing a dark green dress, answered the door.

"I assume you are the woman I spoke with on the phone."

"Yes, I am Pat Lancaster, and this is DK Walker, my assistant."

The lady stepped back, motioning them inside the well-furnished house.

When they were seated, a man in his late seventies dressed in black dress pants and a long-sleeved blue shirt walked across the room to sit in a chair next to the woman.

"Alright, now tell me what is going on with your seemingly out-of-order lamp," Pat said.

The woman looked over at the man and declared with a determined look. "Some time back, we purchased this lamp at an antique shop. For a while, all was fine, and then it began coming on and going off by itself."

"Did you check to see if maybe it had a short?" DK spoke up.

"Of course, I checked it. I found nothing wrong with it," the man told him.

"Can I ask your names?" Pat said.

"My name is Sylvia, and my husband's is Arnold."

"I am glad to meet you. I must place my hands on the lamp to see what I can learn."

"Yes, that will be fine. I must tell you, this is beginning to scare me," Sylvia told them.

"I hate to admit it," Arnold looked over at the lamp, "but it's starting to give me some unease, too."

Pat placed her hands on the lamp and quieted her mind. Instantly, the hideous face of a man leaped into her mind. A high-pitched laugh erupted as he threw back his head. Pat lifted her hands from the lamp and turned to look at the couple seated on the couch.

"Where did you get this lamp?"

"I bought it for Sylvia for Christmas. It is

a beautiful lamp, and I knew she would enjoy having it lit up on the bedside table."

"Pat is asking where you bought the lamp," DK said.

"I bought it from the old antique shop here in town."

"The one on Belair," DK said.

"Yeah, that shop's been here for over thirty years."

"Have you ever purchased anything other than the lamp from the antique shop?"

"No. They have such lovely things in the store. I am surprised we haven't purchased anything over the years. I am a collector of antiques." Sylvia told them.

"Sometimes the people who owned the item earlier can get attached and don't like seeing it belong to a stranger."

"Oh, Good Lord! Are you telling us the lamp is haunted?" Sylvia cried out

"I'm afraid so. The lamp is haunted by a man who looks to be quite elderly."

"What do you advise we do? I am sure the shop will not refund my money. They will laugh and order me from the shop if I tell them I am returning the lamp because a Psychic told me it is haunted."

"I'm afraid you're right. I see you have a pile of leaves raked up. Do you put them into a bin to be hauled off, or do you burn them?"

"I burn them. Why?"

"I think burning the lamp would be a good idea."

"I shouldn't ask, but I like to know why things happen," Sylvia says.

For a moment, Pat remained silent, then, taking a deep breath, walked back over to the lamp. This time, she lifted the lamp into her hands to carry it back to sit in a chair she had moved away from the other people in the room.

"I want everyone to remain seated and quiet. She took several deep breaths to relax her mind and waited to see the man she had seen earlier.

Pat opened her eyes as she felt someone standing beside the chair.

"Who are you?" she asked, silently sending her thoughts to the hideous fantom glaring at her.

"You should not tempt me. My spirit has dwelled in this lamp and has been in this house for many months. You will leave here."

"No. I will not allow you to haunt this couple. You are not a spirit; I can see you have not entered the Light of the Holy Father. You are a ghost, and it is time your reign here ends."

"I will destroy you," He screamed, making everyone in the house jump to their feet.

Pat threw the lamp to the floor and rose

from the chair to confront the threat to her life, standing in the room for all to see.

"I want everyone to walk outside. I am in no danger and can handle this alone."

"The two of you do as Pat has requested. I will remain here," DK tells them.

As Sylvia followed Arnold out the back door, DK stood quietly watching Pat.

"Why are you haunting this lamp? You are not a Genie who does good; I see you as a demon whose only wish is to harm."

"I will take over your soul and deliver you to Satan."

"Before you do this, I am still waiting to hear how you were able to haunt this lamp."

"The lamp dwelled in the church of Satan. He gave his blessing that allowed anyone who worshiped him to be able to inhabit the lamp after their death and bring other souls who purchased the lamp to join Satan in hell. You will not stop me from doing what I am meant to do. Claw-like hands reached out to pull Pat into their grasp.

Pat turned away, calling on the Holy Spirits to destroy the demon and take him to hell.

Sharp screams filled the air as the Spirits wrapped the evil one in chains and disappeared from her sight.

"I guess we can consider this a done removal," DK pulled Pat into his arms for a quick hug.

Pat picked up the lamp and walked out of the house with DK.

Sylvia and Arnold walked forward. Arnold took the lamp Pat handed to him.

"Everything is over and safe now. You will burn this lamp."

Arnold handed Sylvia the lamp and, reaching into his back pants pocket, pulled out his billfold and a check to hand over to Pat.

"Thank you for all your help."

"You both have a great rest of the day," Pat told them as she walked hand in hand with DK to the car.

CHAPTER TWO

"I must say, I was very glad you were here today. Your presence gave me added courage."

"You can rest easy. I will be there any time you need me. I am glad Phil thought of this."

"Phil was worried you and I would split up. He knows we love each other and does not want this love to end."

"I think he can put his worries at ease. I will not do anything to interfere while you are using your God-given gift to put an end to evil. As you showed me again, I know that when evil threatens you, the Holy Ones are there to protect you and take the evil away."

The ringing of DK's cell phone interrupted anything else they had to say on the subject.

"Walker."

"Yeah, DK, Phil here. I received a call that will definitely need both of you to investigate. Can you meet me at 1531 Stratford Rd? This needs attention right now."

"We'll be there in a few minutes." DK turned off the cell.

"Now, what needs our attention?"

"Phil didn't say. Said this is a real bad one.

"They all are, DK. Trust me."

***

As she stopped the car, Pat saw Phil walk out of a three-story blue house.

"Glad to see you wasted no time in getting here," Phil said as Pat and DK exited the car.

"What is going on?"

" A youngin who looks to be no older than ten years old has been murdered in a most foul way."

DK lights a cigarette and then looks away.

Phil does not miss his movement.

"Being an officer on the police force, I am sure you have seen your share of brutal murders, but I have to tell you, I believe this is a first."

"Is the family still in the house?"

"Yeah, Pat, I hate to say they are."

A man in his early forties, dressed in blue jeans and a black pullover, opened the door to usher them inside.

"Mr. Blondell, this is Pat Lancaster and her partner, DK Walker. Pat is a psychic who helps the different police precincts solve cases."

The man stepped back, throwing up his hands.

"No! I do not want this evil in my house! She can leave right now, or all of you will be thrown out!"

Before Phil could say anything, DK stepped in front of Pat.

"Lieutenant Abbot has hired Pat Lancaster to help investigate what happened here. This is a crime scene. You will not threaten Miss Lancaster or anyone in this investigation."

"I have to agree with Officer Walker. Now we are ready to see the body."

Pat pulled Phil off to the side.

"I don't trust that man. It seems to me he is afraid of what I might find. I think you'd better call for backup."

"I think you're right," Phil told her before walking outside.

"Mr. Blondell, I am sorry for what you are so obviously suffering. I am not evil. My psychic gift is given to me by God. I am here to help you."

"I said I do not need your help. Now, get out of my way. I am going to go upstairs and lie down."

Before he could move, DK flipped him around to cuff his hands behind his back. "I know you are grieving, but I am not going to chance your doing anyone harm."

"Thanks, DK. You are making the right move. Backup's on the way," Phil told him, walking back into the house.

"I'm ready to see the body," Pat said.

Pat walked into a large, well-decorated bedroom. She could see the outline of a body on the bed. She moved forward and then inhaled a deep breath. What she saw was so grotesque she had to look away.

"Oh my God in heaven. How could anyone be this evil?"

"It took one sick son of a bitch to do this, Pat, and from the way Blondell was acting, he may be the one we're talking about."

Pat forced her feet to move forward until she was standing beside the mutilated body of a nude female. Her head had been severed and laid off to the side of one of her shoulders. As Pat gazed into the girl's face, she saw the horror staring out of her open eyes. Breathing deeply to relax, she touched the girl's arm. Within moments, the vision of a young man in his mid-teens dressed in jeans and a white T-shirt stood quietly by the bed, staring down at the young girl curled up in the bed, completely unaware of his presence. She listened as she heard him begin to speak.

"Carla, you are my sister, and I love you, but I must do what my mind tells me to do. I can't help the sickness that lives inside me. Daddy knows I can't help what I do, and he made sure we kept no cats or dogs here after he saw what I did to the cats and dogs we had as pets. I was only seven."

The girl opened her eyes and started to scream. He reached out, placing one hand over her mouth.

"You must be quiet so you won't wake Mama and Daddy. I don't want to suffer another whipping like the last time Daddy saw what I did to the neighbor's dog. He should not have hurt me. He should have pitied me instead of beating me."

For a moment, he removed his hand from Carla's mouth and reached over to the night table to pull forth a large knife.

"Donny, you don't want to do this. You are sick. Mama and Daddy need to put you in a mental hospital where you can get help."

"You Bitch. I am not crazy! I am sick! All I hear is how terrible I am and how they wish I had never been born. But they dote on you. Oh, Carla is so pretty and so bright! Well, guess what? They won't think you are so pretty when I get through with you."

He shoved her head back, and with one quick swipe of the sharp knife, the warm blood he craved poured out to cover his hands and soak into the bed. He leaned forward, enjoying his fill and smiling as his heart pounded excitedly.

The vision ended as Pat stepped back, inhaling deep breaths and trying not to vomit.

"I don't know about you, but if I don't get out of here, I'm gonna puke," DK said, turning to walk out of the room.

"Yes, I am ready to leave. I know what happened, and this nightmare has to be brought to an end."

As Pat and DK walked outside, Phil and three police officers moved forward.

"I hope you could find out who the hell did this," Phil said.

"Yes. Who else did you find in the house besides Blondell?"

"A woman, whom I'm assuming is Mrs. Blondell, and a teenage male."

"Where are they now?"

"When I told them that since this is a crime scene, they would have to vacate the house. The woman said she and the boy would go to her mother's house until we were through investigating what happened."

"I hope to hell you had sense enough to get the address, Phil," DK spoke up.

For a moment, Phil drew back, staring at him. "Do I look like a complete idiot to you, Walker? Of course, I got the address."

"It was the girl's brother who committed the murder. Since the parents know the boy is a dangerous psychopath, they can blame themselves for allowing this to happen. I hope the Prosecuting Attorney on the case sees a way of holding them accountable. The way I see it, they aided and abetted the killer."

"I agree. That explains why Blondell wanted you out of here so fast. He knew as a psychic, you would be able to tell what happened and who is to blame."

"I agree, and Phil? One more thing. Thank you for allowing DK to be with me on future cases. This is the worst case I have ever witnessed, and I have to say, were I alone seeing all that happened in that house, I don't think I could have stayed to find out all I needed to know."

DK pulled her against his hip. "I'll always be there for you, Pat."

"Let's go home, DK. I need to be where love grows instead of hate."

On the ride home, DK remained silent for a while, trying to understand how what he had just witnessed could happen. "How does a person become a psychopath?"

Pat glanced over at him. "I can understand what you are feeling. I am wondering the same thing. She was his sister. It doesn't matter that she was the one the parents doted on. In fact, it is understandable. As sick and evil as he is, it's no wonder."

"I'm trying to understand how a person becomes a psychopath?"

"Some psychologists refuse to say that it

is a mental illness."

"How the hell can it not be? A person does not harm animals or humans and not be a sick son of a bitch!"

"I agree. I have never had much faith in what a head doctor can determine."

"That makes two of us." Pat laughs.

"Here we are talking about the sicko, and when we left to come home, we figured on relaxing with a drink and playing with the pups. And cross our fingers the phone doesn't ring, calling us to go to another police mess."

" Are you sorry you came with me today?"

"I'm sure you didn't want to be there any more than I did, but I am glad I was there."

"I'm glad you were there too, DK."

As Pat drove up the driveway, they could hear the welcoming barks inside the house.

"Someone knows we're home," DK said as they stepped to the driveway.

"They are no happier about our being home than we are."

"What do you say after we enjoy a drink and relax, we grab the pups and head off to the park?"

"Sounds like a winner to me."

Ash and Stormy jumped up on the couch, one on each side of DK, to give him a wet kiss on his cheeks.

"I think they like your idea," Pat told him, setting his drink on the end table before motioning the pups to get off the couch so she could sit down.

"This is enjoyable. You brought closure to a very evil murder, and I was able to be by your side. Now we are home and seated beside one another instead of arguing and trying to get the other to quit their job so they can be safe."

"The way I look at this is that we are lending each other strength and showing that in that strength is love and certainty, and we know what we are doing is right."

"Very well put." He lifted his glass in the air. "Now, I will bring up something we haven't discussed in a long time."

"You don't need to get down on your knees. I'll marry you."

DK turned to stare at her. "You always know what is on my mind." He laughed aloud, then jumped to his feet.

"You mean it? You will marry me?"

"I just said I would. Do you want me to put it in writing?"

"Not necessary. Oh my God. I am so happy."

Hearing the excitement in his voice, Ash and Stormy began to dance around the room.

"You two will not be little bastards anymore. Mamma and Daddy are going to get married."

"That drink must have gone to your head." Pat stood up to walk to the kitchen, only to be swung around as DK grabbed her around the waist.

"Let's go in the kitchen and pour us a celebratory drink."

"I think that is a great idea. We'll pour the babies a bowl of milk to join us. I know with the excitement they are seeing and feelin', they are as happy as we are."

They both stop midway to the kitchen as Pat's cell phone rings.

"Happy time just came to a screeching halt," DK growled.

Pat glanced at the name on the phone and then pushed the button. "Hello, Phil. Surprised to hear from you again."

"I knew you and DK would want to know we picked up the boy's parents. I think there is a lot we need to find out about their involvement in all this."

"I agree. I want to know when the psycho started mutilating animals and if we have any proof of his turning that need on children and older humans, since we both know they don't stop."

"Would you and DK like to join me at the station? They should be bringing them in within a half hour."

"Let me talk it over with DK and get back to you, Phil. Thanks for thinking of including us."

"Okay, now what requires our expertise?"

"The parents of the psycho have been picked up. Phil wants to know if we want to meet him at the station in a few minutes."

"Oh hell yes, we do."

"Now, don't go off on a bitch, but I know how angry you can get, so can you keep your anger in check while we're in front of the parents?"

"I'm sure I can. Why? Because I feel they

own a lot of the blame for not getting their son into a mental hospital. I agree that a psycho can't be cured; however, I believe they can be medicated to stop some of their rage."

"So then we need to get the babies situated with food and water and let them out for a few minutes so we don't come home to a pile."

***

Phil motioned them inside his office.

"They aren't here yet, but they shouldn't be long. I want you to sit near the mother and, without being obvious, brush her arm or sleeve to make contact and see what she knows about all this and his years of growing up."

"I can do that. I am curious about the mother's involvement, too. Since you should still have the dad in custody, will he be brought in with the mother and the son?"

"No, I want to talk with him alone. I don't want him to talk over his wife in case she tries to say something that will get him in deeper than he already is."

"Smart move."

A police officer tapped on the door and then ushered a teenage boy dressed in blue jeans and a gray hoodie. The woman walking beside him looked to be in her late forties with dark brown hair worn short and dressed in a pair of black slacks and a pink button-up long-sleeved blouse.

Phil stood up from his chair and pulled out two chairs for them to be seated.

"Before we start, would either of you like something to drink?"

"Yeah, I would. A cold beer and some crack to relax me." The teen said with a smug grin.

"I think you are already in enough trouble. Trying to be cool and bringing drugs and liquor into the conversation is only making things worse for you," Phil told him.

Pat leaned to the side, rubbing the top of

her leg. Her movement brushed the shoulder of the woman seated beside her.

"Now, Mrs. Blondell, how long has your son had a mental illness?" Phil inquired.

"What the hell are you talking about?" The teen jumped to his feet. "I do not have a mental illness. Tell them, Mama. Tell them I am not crazy."

DK came forward, placed a firm hand on the boy's shoulder, and sat him back in his chair.

"You can either stay seated, or you can be taken back to the jail cell. It's up to you." DK refused to look away as the boy stared up at him.

"Now, Mrs. Blondell, I will ask you again, how long have you known your son has a very dangerous mental illness?"

"You go to hell! I want to leave here right now! Do you hear me? Right now!"

Phil pushed a button to call the outside

desk. "Lanore, have someone bring me a chair for the male just brought in for questioning. Thank you."

"I want my dad. Bring my dad here. He'll tell you I am not crazy."

"Donny," his mother said, "you need to sit down and behave."

"Fuck you, old lady! I should have cut off your head, too. I hate you! Did you hear what I said? I hate you!"

"Yes, Donny, I heard you, just as I have heard you since you could talk," she whispered, rubbing a hand across her eyes.

"Your mother heard you; more importantly, we listened to what you said. You're under arrest for first-degree murder."

Phil motioned the officer forward, standing outside his office. "As soon as the chair is brought in and we have him strapped in, you can take him downstairs and put him back in a cell. I am sure he was read his rights, but read his rights to him again to be on the safe side."

"We thought, with a lot of love and keeping no pets on the property, that Donnie would get over his need to do harm. I can see now we were wrong."

"I'm no doctor, but I would guess your son is a psychopath. He should have been put in a mental hospital years ago."

"I wanted to; however, his father fought me on getting that done. He said no son of his could have a mental illness."

"Sounds like his father could have done with some mental help himself," DK spoke up, then looked away as Pat glanced over at him.

"Donny's father has always been ashamed of Donny. Calling him names and slapping him around."

"When did you first notice Donny wanting to harm animals?"

"He was about five years old. I entered

the room where my sister's baby was sleeping in her bassinet. I saw Donnie slap her, making her cry, and I ran over and stopped him from hitting her again."

"What did Donnie do when you stopped him from hitting her again?"

"He looked at me and began laughing."

"I told him he was a bad boy for hitting the baby and that he was never to do that again."

"When did harming animals come into play?"

"He was caught drowning the neighbor's kittens."

"Well, maybe now he can get some help. He will be admitted to a mental hospital and put on drugs. Then he will go on trial, and depending on the judge, he will go to prison or be put back in the mental hospital. Either way, he will not be running free where he can harm others."

Alone in Phil's office, Phil looked over at Pat as she sat quietly in her chair.

"Were you able to glean anything when you brushed against Mrs. Blondell?"

"Yes. Donnie is a psychopath, and his father has known this for years. He has seen the horror Donnie did to animals repeatedly."

"Since this has come to light, I will talk with the Prosecuting Attorney and see what charges can be brought against Blonell. Aiding and abetting is a serious charge. That son of a bitch could have saved his daughter from being murdered."

"I agree with you 100%, Phil."

"I guess we can consider this case solved, and here are both your checks for a job well done."

"Thank you, Phil. I am ready to go home and enjoy a leisurely drink with my man."

"You don't need to ask me twice."

CHAPTER THREE

Pat set her drink on the end table and then turned to look at DK as he sat quietly, staring off into space.

"What did you think of your first day at your new job?"

He rubbed a hand across his eyes and inhaled a deep breath. "That kid is one sick puppy. To kill his own sister in such a cold and callous way speaks of complete evil."

"I agree. A diseased mind leaves those with a healthy and normal mind reaching for answers."

"I don't understand why the parents, when they saw how cruel he was, did not get him checked by a reputable doctor."

"I guess they simply thought that by

ignoring what he was doing, he would stop in time. Mental illness does not stop; it only escalates, putting those around them in danger."

"That sure as hell was the way of it in that family."

"I am all for going to get something…," she stopped what she was saying to answer her cell phone.

"Hello, Phil, what's up?"

"Looks like it will be one of those days when everything falls to ruin. We just got a call about a missing elderly gentleman."

"How long has he been missing?"

"Since late last night. He lives with his daughter, her husband, and their three kids. His daughter wished him goodnight at about 9 p.m., and when he didn't come down for breakfast, she went up to check on him and found him gone."

"Is she at the station now, or will you talk

with her at her house? I'm fine. Let me correct that. We are fine either way."

DK smiled over at her.

"I would rather we meet at her house. You might be able to pick up on something there to help us find him."

"Give me the address, and then we'll see you there in about half an hour."

"Sounds good. Oh, is DK still working with us? After what we went through earlier, I thought he may want to return to his regular beat."

"DK does not give up that easy. We'll see you in a few."

"Sounds like Phil thought I would already be back on the old job. While I do hope we are not going to be dealing with another sick son of a bitch like before, I don't cut and run."

"A man has been missing since late last night. As he is elderly, we may be dealing with someone with Alzheimer's Disease."

That in itself is bad enough. Poor old dude don't know what the hell is going on."

"Maybe. Guess we'll see in a few."

They could see Phil's vehicle parked up the street from the house.

Pat and DK exited the car and walked up the driveway to tap on the front door.

The tall, slender woman who came to the door looked to be in her middle fifties, with long blond hair, dressed in a dark red skirt and a white, long-sleeved silk blouse.

"Hello. Won't you come in? Lieutenant Abbot is already in the living room. Would you like a cup of fresh coffee, and if so, how do you take your coffee?"

"Yes, coffee sounds good and black, please."

Phil gets to his feet as Pat and DK walk into the room. "Here, Pat." He motioned her to sit in his vacated chair. "I think you will be comfortable in this chair. We can all sit on the couch."

"Thank you."

"Mrs. Sutter, this lady is Pat Lancaster, and the gentleman with her is DK Walker. Pat is a psychic who helps different precincts solve cases. I feel certain she can help you locate your father."

"I sure hope so. Dad has not shown any problems pointing to dementia. So, I don't know what is going on."

"How old is your father?"

"He is seventy-five. He has always been very clear-headed."

"Could I possibly go up to his room? Since that was the last place he was, I may be able to pick up on his whereabouts quickly."

"I'll show you his room if you both come with me. I am so nervous I can't stop shaking."

"Understandable," Pat told her.

Pat follows the woman into a very well-kept room to stand looking around. On the table next to the bed, she sees his wallet.

"Odd that if he were to leave the house, you would think he would have taken his wallet with him."

"Yes. Another thing I found odd is he left the lid off his expensive men's cologne in his bathroom."

"Why would he put on men's cologne just before bed?" Pat spoke up.

"Yeah, I thought it strange, too."

"What is your first name?" Pat asked her.

"My name is Hillary."

"Okay, Hillary, do you mind if I go into his bathroom?"

"No. That's fine."

Once in the bathroom, Pat picks up the uncapped bottle of men's cologne. She brings the bottle to her nose. The aroma is very pleasing, making her nod her head in approval. She picks up a hairbrush lying beside the marble sink, glad to see it has not been cleaned of hair. She slowly relaxed her mind, then closed her eyes. A handsome, well-dressed older man with a full head of thick white hair appeared. His dark blue eyes were alert and smiling. He held out his hand to a tall, attractive woman who looked to be in her mid-fifties, dressed in a long cream-colored negligee as she walked towards him, smiling. He drew her into his arms for a long, leisurely kiss on her full mouth before picking her up in his arms to carry her across the room to lay her down on a king-size bed.

"I have looked forward to our being together all day," she whispered in a deep and sexy voice.

"My beautiful Jennifer, you need wait no longer," He told her.

Already knowing where their get-together would end up, Pat opened her eyes, a small laugh filling the room.

She walked out of the room. A smile covered her face as Hillary waited to hear what Pat has to tell her.

"Do you know a woman in her mid-fifties named Jennifer"?

"Why, yes. Jennifer is our neighbor who lives across the street. Why would you ask about Jennifer?"

"Your father is safe. In fact, he is safe in Jennifer's arms."

"Are you telling me my father spent the night with our neighbor Jennifer?"

"Yes. Instead of being shocked and angry, he did not tell you his plans. Be glad he is safe and enjoying himself. Your father is a very handsome man who belies his age."

Pat glanced over at DK as he stood looking at her with a big grin covering his face.

"I guess we can consider this case closed."

"Thank you both for your time."

"No problem, Pat told her. As she turned to leave, she looked back at the young woman watching her. "Hillary, be glad this is how it all turned out for your father. In our work, things rarely turn out for the best."

As they walked outside, DK leaned in close. "I think she should be happy her dad was getting his ashes hauled by a loving woman rather than have his ashes hauled by a coroner."

CHAPTER FOUR

The shrill ringing of Pat's cell phone had DK moaning aloud into the night.

"Aw shit! This can't be good for an uninterrupted night's sleep."

"Hello. This is Pat. Okay, we'll meet you there in a few."

"Now what?"

"That was Phil. An entire family was murdered at 1532 Kimbro Rd. Time to get up and going."

"I'll get the coffee brewing while you get ready, and we can take some with us. I don't like getting up at night, but I sure won't do it without coffee."

"Sounds good. Don't forget to let the babies out and back in."

"Yeah, I can do that."

***

As they rode through the night, Pat tried to relax her mind. She always felt her nerves go into overdrive when a family was destroyed.

"I will never get used to evil and what it can do to the innocent. Nine times out of ten, it is a coward pitting his strength against those who are weaker. It's always a child or a woman. They don't have enough balls to go up against another man."

"I hear you. One of the things I appreciate about my gift is that I can get those bastards found and put away so they can never do something like this again."

"Yeah, if we get the weaklings out of power and office and those with strength voted in."

Pat maneuvered her vehicle behind a police car and shut off the motor.

"With all the cops here, Phil has enough

help."

"Phil knows what he is doing. He is a good man and a great leader."

"I guess it's time to go get another sicko found and put behind bars."

"That's what we're here for."

Pat opens her car door and steps to the pavement.

DK slips an arm around her slender waist as they make their way up to the front door.

"Is it just me, or do you have an eerie feeling?"

"Yes, I do. When evil happens in the dead of night, it is almost like the one committing the evil can hide in the darkness."

"Yeah, I hear you. Here comes Phil. He can fill us in on what we can expect."

"Glad you're here. I hope you both have a strong stomach 'cause this will test you like nothing ever has."

"Sounds like a real mess," DK said.

"Mess is putting it mildly. We have a man, a woman, and three kids, ages eight to two. I tell you, I about threw up, and I've seen a lot of sick murders."

"Are they all in one room or spread out in the house?"

"Spread out. The kids were already in bed."

"Okay, let's get in and see what I can find."

A man and a woman in their early forties lay sprawled out on the floor in the large front room. They had been shot numerous times, and their faces had been kicked so hard that the bones in their faces were utterly shattered.

"This took a real evil son of a bitch entirely out of his mind to have done this."

"How do you know a man did this, DK? Women can have sick minds, too."

"I agree, but I assumed a male did this since children are involved in this filth. I won't call him a man since he is not a man but a coward."

"Tell me where the children are, and I will see what I can find out. You both can wait downstairs if you like."

"I'll wait here," Phil told her. "The older children are in the first two bedrooms at the top of the stairs, and the baby is in the main bedroom further down the hall."

"I'll come with you, Pat, if this is all right."

"Yes, I would like you to be with me."

The door to the first bedroom was standing open. Pat breathed a deep breath to steel herself for what was to come. She saw a young boy lying atop the covers wearing Spiderman pajamas. His head was blown entirely off his neck and lying beside the bed.

"Good God Almighty," Pat whispered, standing just inside the room. "How the hell could a human do this to another human, especially a child?"

"I am wondering the same thing."

She turned and walked out of the room.

They found the same sick scene involving another child as they stood gazing into the next room.

"I have to tell you, DK. Not that one child is more important than another, but I am going to find it very difficult to look at a murdered baby."

"I hear you. However, we both have a job to do, so let's get it done to find out who did this and then get out of here."

Pat walked forward until she stood beside a crib with a small child drenched in blood with a bullet hole in the middle of his chest.

"I guess the evil bastard did this quickly."

Taking a deep breath, Pat reached out to

place one hand atop the child's head. Within moments, a woman in her mid-sixties, holding a small handgun, came into view. The look on her face as she stood looking at the small child she had just murdered showed a wide smile.

"Believe it or not, DK, this horrendous murder was done by a woman in her sixties. The smile on her face tells me she has no conscience, a complete Schiopath."

"Guess we'd better see if she did all five murders or if there is someone else running outside instead of inside the mental hospital."

Pat knelt, taking the slender woman's hand in hers. Within moments, just like before, the same very unattractive woman she had seen earlier came into her mind's eye. Pat waited to see if she could hear a conversation between the woman and her killer.

"Sarah, why are you doing this? Michael and I love each other. We have a family together. What you had with Michael is long over. Find you someone you can share your life with."

"I don't want anyone else, you sick bitch. Michael was my husband. Do you hear me? Michael...was my... husband!"

A bullet left the gun with each word she said until all was quiet. With the same sick smile, she kicked the face of the man, no longer moving on the floor, and, turning, she walked upstairs to finish what she had come to accomplish.

"The woman who did all of the murders is the ex-wife of the murdered man. Let's go downstairs and let Phil know so he can have her picked up and sent away for five counts of first-degree murder."

"You don't have to ask me twice. The sooner we are out of here, the better."

CHAPTER FIVE

"I am very impressed with Phil's decision to pay you to be with me on the cases the precincts need to solve. It saves them money and prevents them from wasting time checking out the different leads."

"I'm glad he thought of having me earn a living accompanying you. We work well together, and it also stops our unneeded anger."

"The woman who murdered that entire family had me wanting to walk away from this case. I have never felt that way before. I have investigated many sick cases, but this one was at the top of the heap of evil."

"What made you decide you needed to stay and discover what happened, and who did such a terrible evil?"

"I felt your presence there with me. It gave me the strength to continue doing what I needed to do."

DK looked at her and reached out, gently touching her shoulder. "You, my darling, just made my day."

"I will let Phil know we need a break for at least one day, maybe two. Any sick individuals who can't control themselves can stay unknown for a few hours. I know such mentally ill urges need to be stopped as soon as possible, but I need a break."

"I'm sure Phil will understand. You have been going nonstop for quite some time. I know he would rather you stop for a while rather than burn out."

"As we always say, what we want to do but get interrupted before we can, let's pick up our fur babies and go for a long walk."

"I think that is a great idea. They have been ignored for too long."

Pat pulled the car into the driveway and turned off the ignition.

"Do we want to fix a picnic lunch to take with us? We haven't done that in forever, either."

"How about we stop and pick up some fast food? We can get Stormy and Ash their favorites, too."

Pat's cell phone began to ring, causing a look of annoyance on both their faces.

"I guess now we find out if Phil will go along with our being out of the cleanup of any messes in the precinct for a few days."

"Hello, Phil," Pat said on the phone, then listened to what he had to say.

"DK and I have decided to take a few days off from all the murder and mayhem. After what we went through with the murders of an entire family, I need a break. Can you and your department investigate this in the old-fashioned way this time? It would be appreciated if you can."

DK stood watching Pat and waiting for her to tell him what was happening.

"Thanks, Phil. I'll talk with you in a few days."

"What's happening they can't deal with now?"

"A robbery at the small grocery store a few blocks from the station."

"I'm sure he wasn't thrilled when you told him we would not be there for a few days."

"I think he took the news surprisingly well."

"Okay, then let's get the hell out of here with no phones and enjoy our day."

Walking in the fresh air with the furbabies running up ahead, Pat could feel the strength she needed to enter back in to wash away the weakness that had been trying to overpower her.

"This is what I needed. I have so much strength now that I could whip the entire world if needed."

DK smiled over at her. "If you have that much overflowing energy, perhaps we should return home and work it off."

Pat laughed outright. "Nice try, Romeo. We will enjoy this fresh air and allow the babies to enjoy being out with us."

"Okay, but remember I offered."

"I know. You always think of me and want only the best you have to offer."

"I'm glad you can see," he breathed, the smile spreading across his face disappearing as he gazed up ahead, "what the hell is that?"

Pat stopped to look at what he was seeing."Looks like a body."

"I swear to Pete, if we don't find a case to investigate, it finds us."

They stopped beside the all-but-nude body of a young woman. Her manner of death was apparent in the blood covering her throat.

"And we don't even have a phone to call Phil and let him know about this."

"This path doesn't look well traveled, so I doubt anyone else will come here. I guess we can head back home and get the pups settled. After we call this in, I'm sure Phil and the coroner will want us to meet them back here."

"So much for our relaxing afternoon with the fur babies."

CHAPTER SIX

Pat sits quietly on the sofa with Stormy beside her, thinking about her relationship with DK. Now that he could be with her while she investigated the wrongdoings, she was called to find out about made a difference in their relationship.

"Looks as though someone is deep in thought. Am I anywhere in those thoughts"?

"You are never far from my thoughts, DK. You should know this by now. I feel our relationship has taken a turn for the better."

"I agree. Now that I can be near you when evil has reared its ugly head, it makes me feel much stronger. I'm a man, and as a man, it is my place to keep you safe." He says, dropping beside her on the couch and laughing as Stormy gives him an angry look before jumping to the floor.

"I love you so very much, DK."

He reached out, taking her into his arms to hold her close against his chest.

"Does this mean we can get back to planning a wedding?"

"Yes."

"Do we want this wedding in the backyard or a chapel?"

"It is your choice, my love."

DK leans back, stretching his legs out straight. "I will need to give this some thought. While I would be just as happy standing with you before a Justice of the Peace, I still want others to share our happy day and envy me." He burst out laughing as Pat slaps him on the arm.

"I know I want Phill as my best man. Do you know who you will choose for your matron of honor?"

"No, I don't. I don't really have any best friends."

"As smart and helpful as you are, that is hard to believe."

Pat picks up her cell and looks down at the caller's name as it rings. "Hello, Phill, were your ears burning?"

"No, but I thought you and DK would be interested in hearing what we found out about the young woman you found murdered. We can get to why my ears should have been burning later."

"Yes. What did you find out about her?"

"Her name was Katland, and she was the Mayor's daughter. You can be sure he will want you to investigate this one."

"How long had she been missing?" I did not think she had been dead long when we came across her body."

"According to Mayor Sandusky, she was not missing. He thought she was in Georgia with her sister. When he received a call from her sister asking why she was not answering her phone, he became concerned and called the Sheriff's Department. I asked him to describe his daughter; sure enough, it was the girl you and Dk found."

"DK and I will meet you at the morgue in about an hour."

"See you then."

Pat clicks off the phone to lay it on the coffee table.

"The girl we found was the Mayor's daughter. As you heard, we will meet Phill at the morgue in an hour."

***

"I will step out with Doctor Markis here to give you the time you need alone with the deceased," Phil said.

Pat walks over to the stainless steel table with the body of the young woman in question. She breathes deeply, relaxing her mind, and then takes the cold hand of the deceased.

Pat sees the woman in question reach out her arms to a very pretty young woman to draw her into her arms. After a leisurely kiss, they step back to gaze at each other.

"We both know our families are not going to accept our being together," Katland whispered. My father is a mayor; he will be too embarrassed to have a dyke for a daughter."

"I wish you would not use that word. We are two women who are in love with each other. It is our business with whom we have a relationship."

"I agree, Jan, but you don't know my father. He will send me out of the country to keep me away from you when he finds out about us."

"Good. Then we can resume our relationship in another country."

"Please don't make light of this, my love. I have never felt this way about anyone."

Pat inhales a startled breath as she sees a man's face peering at the couple from a grove of trees nearby. She watches as he steps into the clearing and raises a gun.

"Dad," Kateland says, backing away from Jan. "What are you doing here, and how did you know where to find me?"

Her father steps forward, still brandishing the firearm he is holding in his hand.

"I heard about this filthy affair from your sister. I didn't believe you were this evil. I am the Mayor of this city, and I can't afford to have people making fun of me because my own daughter is a dirty dyke."

"With whom I have a love relationship is my business. If you can't accept this, I will move out of the state, and no one will be the wiser."

"Oh, trust me, you will be leaving the state and taking this waste of breath," he looks at Jan, "with you. I haven't struggled all these years to make something of myself to have a daughter of mine come along and destroy it for me."

"You don't care about me or anyone else in the family. You only care about Mayor Daddy and power."

"You ungrateful bitch." He aimed the gun and pulled the trigger. As Kateland fell to the ground, two more shots were heard, dropping Jan beside the unmoving body of Kateland.

Pat tried to calm herself with deep breaths as she saw the man who had ended the lives of two girls draw back a foot and kick each girl in the face. Unable to observe anymore, Pat opened her eyes to leave the room.

Both Phil and DK walked forward as Pat came down the hall.

"Were you able to find out who killed the Mayor's daughter?" Phil spoke up.

"Yes. You will be finding the body of

another young girl, too, as they were both murdered by the same man."

"Were you able to identify the killer?"

"Yes, Dk. The man who killed the girl you and I found was the girl's father. She and the other girl he murdered were having an affair, and the Mayor, being the strong Christian he is, could not allow this."

"Do you know where we can start looking for the second girl?" Phil asked.

"Yes, you will find her not too far from where his daughter's body was found."

***

DK handed Pat a glass of red wine before sitting beside her on the couch.

"It always amazes me how someone can have so few feelings for someone who is their own child. Is money and power really that important?"

"To some, it is. However, they were never

moral in the first place."

CHAPTER SEVEN

DK sips his sweet wine and smiles, enjoying the taste. He looks over at Pat.

"I think it is time we discuss our getting together. Not simply living together, although I must say I have no problem with our sharing the same house and sharing the same bed and being loving parents to our little furbabies, I think it is time we move on to a stronger relationship."

Pat laughs outright. "I guess what you are trying to say is you want a marriage license to tell the world that I belong to you and you belong to me."

"I think that pretty well covers it. And what may I ask, do you think of this well-thought-out idea?"

"I think it is a great idea. Now we have to decide if we want a large wedding or go to the justice of the peace."

"My choice is a wedding in church with all our friends."

"And who is your choice for a best man?"

"Phil, of course. Now, who will you have for your maid of honor?"

"I will have to give that some thought. I have a good friend with whom I have not been in touch for a while. If she wants to be my maid of honor, she will be the one I choose."

"Then you'd best get a hold of her so we can get this show on the road."

"I want our furbabies in the wedding. We will find another church if the preacher won't allow them inside."

"I agree."

"Then I suggest you get ahold of Phil and let him know..." She turned to answer her cell. "Hello, Phil. You must be psychic, as your name came up in DK's and my conversation just now."

"I wish that were the reason, but I need both of you to meet me on Highway 17 and Ash. The house, a little ways off the highway, is white and three-story. When you arrive, I'll fill you in on all the gory details."

"Okay, we'll see you there."

"I'll go tend to the critters," DK said, getting to his feet.

DK slowed the jeep as Pat nodded to the big white house at the end of a long stone driveway.

"Damn! That's one hell of a house. Almost looks like the White House."

"Yeah. Let's hope it doesn't hold as much evil."

DK laughed, stopping behind Phil's vehicle.

Stepping out of the house, Phil waved them forward. "Glad to see you wasted no time getting here."

"What do we have this time?"

"Believe it or not, Pat, I would say we are dealing with another Satanic Cult."

"Oh crap, not those sick fuckers again," DK murmured.

Phil nodded. "Yeah, they don't get any more evil."

"I sure hope no children are involved in their merriment."

"Sorry to tell you, DK, but there are."

"Let's go inside so I can see what is going on," Pat says.

"I'll say one thing. If this doesn't make you sorry you took this job, DK, nothing will."

"Oh, thanks, Phil. If this is going to make me lose the relaxing glass of wine I just enjoyed, maybe I should stay out here and let you two check this one out."

"Come on, DK, I prefer having you beside me."

"That's all I needed to hear, my love." He slips an arm around her waist as they continue inside the house.

Pat drew a deep breath as she felt the evil surround her from all sides.

"I can feel you shaking, Sweetheart."

"There is so much evil here that it is hard to get above it. Everyone here was a believer in Satan."

"Too bad they did not listen when someone tried to tell them that Our Holy Father is stronger than Satan."

"Maybe they were not raised in God's word. Some children aren't, and it is a shame." Phil breathed.

They walked down a flight of stairs leading to a basement where they could see an altar. On the altar was a young female. Her heart had been removed and laid at her feet.

"Took some really sick trash to do this," DK says.

Pat glanced over at him. "They think because they believe in Satan that they are above the law and will never have to spend time in prison for what they do."

"I got news for the son of a bitches, when we find them, they will pay the maximum penalties, and the evil bastard they worship will not be able to do anything about it."

"I agree with you, Phil." DK nods his head.

"How did you come to find out about something being amiss here?"

"We got a call from the neighbor saying they haven't seen anything here. Before, they were always hearing moans and eerie music. But nothing of late."

"Okay, Phil. I will take it from here if you

want to step out in the hall."

"You don't have to ask me twice, Pat," Phil tells her as he walks to the basement stairs.

"First thing we need to do is find out the name of the people who lived here."

Pat nods, then breathes deeply to quiet her thoughts and relax her mind.

She sees children being stabbed and thrown across the floor. One young girl is picked up and laid on the altar.

"You were my daughter, Rebecca, but you would not listen when I told you how important our religion is to this family. Now you will see the one we hold most high as you enter the dark side."

A movement catches her eye, and she sees a tall woman in her early forties dressed in a black robe running out the basement door. She kept her mind's eye on the woman to see where she is and finally has to give up. "I have done all I can do here, DK," she tells him. "But a woman ran out of the basement door and needs to be found."

DK turns, going to the door. "Phil, you need to get back down here," he calls out.

Phil wasted no time returning to the basement.

"What did you find?"

"The children were killed by their father, who, of course, is a satanist. But I saw a woman in her early forties dressed in black robes run out the basement door. You need to get some of your deputies here to locate her. I'm through here, so you can also get ahold of the corner."

"Then I guess you and DK can be on your way, and I will keep you informed of what we find on the woman."

DK and Pat walk out of the house, and DK stops. "I know you are the psychic, but I just had a strong feeling about the woman who ran out of this house."

Pat looks at him. "Tell me what your

feeling is."

"I think she is at the neighbor's house who called in about not seeing anyone there for a long time."

Pat keyed her cell. "Phil, don't leave. You need to call for backup. I want to check out the house across the street. Since this is where we found out about no one seen for quite a while and then found what we did, I think this could be where the woman who ran out of the basement is."

Phil quickly backs his vehicle back into the driveway and calls for backup.

DK follows Pat as she walks over to Phil's vehicle.

"We'll wait for backup before going to the neighbor's house. Who knows, the sick bastard could be holding the people in the house hostage."

As four police cars stop behind Pat's car, Phil pushes his door open and steps onto the driveway.

"Surround the house," he nods to the house across the street."

DK and I will follow you, Phil," Pat says. "I should be able to see what is happening inside when we get on the property."

DK, along with Phil, draws their weapons before walking forward.

Pat knocks on the door, and within moments, a short, stocky woman in her late sixties dressed in black slacks and a white top answers the door.

"Yes?" she looks at them.

Phil pulls her out of the house.

"Is anyone else in the house?" he asks.

"Yes," she says, her voice shaking with fear. The man and woman who live across the street are inside. He has been beating and kicking the woman."

"Is anyone else in the house?"

She shakes her head back and forth.

"Do you know if he has a gun?"

"I didn't see a gun. He keeps beating his wife. He told me to sit down and shut up, or he would beat me too. I did what he told me to do."

Phil and DK walked inside the house.

"You need to come out with your hands up. We know you're in here. We will loose the dogs on you if you don't come outside now."

A tall man in his late fifties walks through the open door with his hands in the air.

"You're under arrest for murder," Phil tells him as one of the deputies grabs his hands behind his back and cuffs him.

The woman Pat saw who ran out of the basement comes forward and runs over to her neighbor, who pulls her into her arms in a tight hug.

"Oh my god, I was so frightened. He was

acting like a lunatic, killing our children and beating me. I ran out of the house. He came after me, screaming for me to stop and come back."

"You're safe now, Rhonda. Raymond can't hurt you anymore."

"Thank you for calling the police, Jenny," she tells the woman, still holding her close.

"I wish I had called earlier. Maybe we could have saved the children."

"Don't beat yourself up over that. He was an evil son-of-a-bitch," Phil told her.

He turns to Pat and Dk. "I'll get the corner out here to take over. You and DK can go home. And thanks for all your help."

Pat gives him a quick hug. "All you have to do is call, and we'll be here."

DK shakes Phil's hand before walking across the street to head home.

CHAPTER EIGHT

Pat sets down her freshly filled cup of coffee to lift her ringing cell to her ear.

"Hello."

"Hello. I was given your name and number by Phil Abbot to call. I am in need of a psychic."

"All right, and your name is?"

"My name is Cindy Lou. I can't come to your house as I don't drive, so can you meet me at the Road Stop Café?"

"Okay, Cindy Lou, I will see you along with my partner, DK, at the café within the hour."

"Sounds like someone is being spooked."

"Yes. I guess we can also enjoy lunch

while we are at the café. They have excellent food there."

"I am starting to get hungry. I'll see to the fur babies, and then we can be on our way."

***

As they walked into the café, they could see a young woman who looked to be in her early twenties, dressed in a white dress and seated at a table.

When she sees Pat and DK, she raises her hand to greet them.

"Guess she's the one we're here to see," DK says quietly.

"Hello, Cindy Lou."

"Hello. Please be seated."

When a middle-aged waitress approached the table, Pat told her what she and DK wanted to eat.

"Did you already have lunch?" DK looked over at her.

"No, but that is fine. I am not hungry."

"Oh, come on now. I won't be comfortable eating in front of you."

"We will treat you to lunch," Pat told her.

"Okay, then I will have what the two of you have for lunch."

DK signaled the waitress to come back to their table and told her she needed to get another order for them.

"Now, Cindy Lou, why don't you fill us in on what is going on that you need our help with?"

Okay, but first, I want to tell you that I don't have any money, but I will gladly come to your house and clean."

"Don't worry. We can forgo any payment. Now, what is going on?"

"A few months ago, a good friend of mine died. To tell the truth," she smiled and turned away momentarily, "Gene and I were lovers."

"All right," Pat said. "Please continue."

"I feel uncomfortable telling you about Gene because he was married."

"Cindy Lou, we are not here to judge you. We are here to help you."

Cindy Lou takes a deep breath and sits back in her chair. "You don't know how good that makes me feel."

Their waitress walks up to their table to place their lunch orders on the table in front of them.

"I will be right back to freshen your coffee."

"Thank you," Pat tells her.

DK watches Cindy Lou as she begins eating.

In between bites, she tells them what they are waiting to hear.

"A while after Gene died, I started noticing that the laces of my shoes were tied in a bow every morning. I knew I didn't do this, so it was beginning to freak me out."

"I can see where it would," DK says.

Cindy Lou glances at him, then goes back to eating her lunch.

"I guess I am trying to say that I believe Gene is haunting me. I do find this hard to fathom as he never mistreated me in any way all the time we were together, and he knew I frightened easily."

"Pat looked at her and smiled. "He is not trying to frighten you. He is telling you he loves and misses you."

"He has a strange way of showing it. If this is the way he wants to show me he still loves and misses me, he can do this by leaving me the hell alone."

"Then here is what you will have to do, Cindy Lou. When you go home, you will say aloud, Gene, in the name of the Holy light of Jesus Christ, I demand you leave me alone."

Cindy Lou dropped her fork on her plate and looked at Pat.

"Do you really believe this will work?"

"I know it will work. While Gene is not coming to you to frighten you, the fact remains he is, and you, as a child of God, have the right to send him away."

A bright smile spread across Cindy Lou's pretty face.

"I am ready to go home right now and put your advice into motion, Pat. I thank you both for taking the time to help me."

Pat and DK stood up and, with a bright smile, made their way to pay the bill before walking out the door of the café.

CHAPTER NINE

"I think we should get back to deciding where we want to marry."

"Yeah, before the damn cell takes off again."

"I am all for the Justice of The peace. I will call around and see what all we need, and if we need a matron of honor, then I don't know who to call."

"I know I can call on Phil for my best man if one is needed."

"Maybe Phil's wife would be my matron of honor."

"Without a shadow of a doubt, you just found the one we need," he pulled her into his arms for a big hug and a quick kiss.

"Okay, since we don't want this invitation

to be secondhand, I will call her right now."

Pat reached out for her cell lying on the coffee table, but it began to ring before she could pick it up.

"Hello."

"Hello, Pat; I hope I am not interrupting anything important."

"Hi, Phil. No, we're just sitting here contemplating marriage and who we need as our Matron of Honor and Best Man. Do you think you or the Mrs. would be interested?"

"I can make a quick phone call and find out for you."

"That would be greatly appreciated. I know you didn't call to chit-chat, so what's up?"

"Yeah, I just got a call from a man saying his girlfriend is missing. Thought we might as well get on it."

"Give me the address and Dk, and I can

meet you there in about a half hour."

"Sounds good. See you then, and I'm sure I'll have found your Matron of Honor by then."

Pat turns off the phone and sets it on the coffee table.

Phil says we have a missing person and that he will speak to the Mrs. about being at the wedding."

"Let me see to the kids, and we can be on our way." He gets to his feet and walks toward the back door.

***

DK pulls into the driveway of the address Phil had given them.

"Here comes Phil," Pat says.

As the two get out of the car, Phil takes DK's hand in a firm handshake.

"The man we are here to talk with is named Lester Hicks. I didn't tell him about bringing the two of you here to talk with him; I want to hear what he has to say before I let him know I am involving a psychic."

"You are a smart man, Phil."

"I do my best to stay on top of things, Pat," he smiles at her.

The three walk up to the front door, and Phil reaches out and rings the doorbell.

A tall and very skinny man in his late 30s, dressed in oversized black slacks and a white T-shirt, answers the door.

"Yeah, what?"

"Hello, Mr. Hicks, I am Detective Phil Abbot, and this is Pat Lancaster and DK Walker. We are here to talk with you about a missing person."

"I don't think we need to involve anyone else in this. I called the police station to speak with a detective, and one detective is all I care to talk to."

"Let's all go inside, and you can fill us in on what is going on."

Lester gives them a sneering look, then backs up to usher them inside.

Hicks pulled out a chair at the small kitchen table and motioned them to be seated. They waited for him to tell them what was going on.

"Now, Mr. Hicks, what can we do to help you?"

"My girlfriend, Jeanine, is missing. She was supposed to meet me last night to go to dinner, but never showed."

"Have you tried calling her? Maybe she is ill."

"She doesn't answer her phone. This is not like her. I am just scared out of my mind that something has happened to her."

"All right. Do you have something of hers, such as a comb or toothbrush? If you have a comb, do not remove the hair."

"What in the hell would you need her comb for?"

Mr. Hicks, Miss Lancaster is a psychic. She helps the department solve cases."

***

"What the hell are you talking about? I don't need a damn psychic. I need a cop to figure out what is happening here."

Pat stood up. "Mr. Hicks, I am sorry, but can I use your bathroom?"

"Yeah, it is down the hall, the first door on the right."

"Okay, now Mr. Hicks…"

"Would you call me Lester? You make me sound like a doddering old man."

"Yes, I can do that. So, Lester," Phil scoots back his chair and leans forward, "I need to ask you a few questions."

"Of course. Ask me anything you want. I want to get onto finding my Jeanine."

"Have you and Janine had any arguments or fighting recently?"

"No. We are very much in love and always have kind words."

"My next question will sound strange, but it is routine when a loved one is missing."

Lester began to move around and wiped a hand over his face in a nervous manner.

"Am I making you nervous?"

"No, not at all. I slept poorly last night, and I am worried about Jeanine."

Pat walked into the room and pulled her chair over next to Lester. She boldly reached out, taking one of his hands in hers.

"What the hell are you doing?" He yanked his hand away from her, "And what are you doing with Jeanin's hairbrush?"

"Pat Lancaster is a psychic. The questions I am asking are being asked to help you."

"Is there a reason you do not want me to

take your hand, Lester?"

"I don't need to be coddled. I want to get on with your finding, Jeanine. If you can't do this without grabbing onto me, you can get out, and I'll find someone else to help."

DK gets to his feet to stand in front of Lester.

"You need to calm down. You asked for help. We are here to help you. You have no reason to run your mouth in a surly manner."

"Sorry," he murmured, looking at Pat as she sat with her eyes closed and holding the hairbrush.

"Lester, when you were asked earlier if you and Jeannie have had any arguments or fighting recently, you said no; however, I see you slapping her in anger."

"All right, yes, we did have a spat a week ago, and my anger got out of hand, so I slapped her. But that was the first and only time." He ran a hand over his face.

"Do you see how this looks to us, Lester? Your girlfriend is missing, and you just admitted you slapped her. Could you have done more than slap her? Sometimes, in anger, a person can get out of control quickly and do more than they meant."

Lester jumps to his feet. "I think I made a big mistake in calling the police. I would appreciate it if you would leave now."

"It is not going to be that simple, Lester. A woman is missing, and you have admitted to abusing her. You will need to come with us to the station to answer some questions."

"I said you need to leave my house. Are you so stupid you can't understand when you have been told to leave?"

DK pulls a set of handcuffs attached to the back of his belt and flips Lester around to cuff both his hands.

"You're going to come with us, Lester. I am sure some questions need to be answered."

"You son of a bitch! You will get these cuffs off me right now!"

"You have quite a temper, Lester. Did Jeanine have the misfortune to bring that temper forward?"

"That filthy pig! She kept running her mouth. I told her to shut up! That I am the one in control of this relationship. But she just kept right on screeching. Well," he laughed, "she knows now that she should have obeyed."

"You killed her. I can see you putting your hands around her throat and squeezing until she was dead. Now, you need to tell us where we can find her body," Pat says.

"She is upstairs in our bedroom. All the crazy bitch had to do was shut the hell up and do her duty of satisfying my needs."

Upon the arrival of the deputies and the corner, DK ushered the corner inside the house and Hicks over to the police car to let the deputy uncuff his hands and hand the cuffs over to DK before pulling his own cuffs forward.

"Guess this is another solved case."

Smiling, DK pulls her against his hip as they walk down the driveway.

CHAPTER TEN

Pat sits alone in the darkness, staring out the window as she tries to shut out the thoughts running nonstop through her mind.

Why had she given in to DK about their getting married? She could not give him children. With his giving personality and ability to flavor the day with laughter and make the right decisions in their, more often than not, work environment, she knew he would want to be a father.

The sharp ringing of her cell breaks into her thoughts. She pulls the phone forward and presses the on button.

"Hello."

"Hi, Pat. Sorry for the late call, but a man at the station, Jonathan Reems, insists that his house is haunted."

"This is nothing new, Phil. Why are you getting upset?"

"I am getting upset," his tone of voice becomes angry, "because the man in my office says his house is haunted by a male ghost who told him that if he does not welcome him into his home, he will kill the entire family."

"Sounds as though you have a mentally disturbed man who needs to be taken to a mental hospital. Since he is already there, why are you not calling someone to come pick him up?"

"To tell you the truth, I don't know why I am not having him picked up. It is almost as though I believe he is telling the truth."

"Okay, before I wake DK and we come to the station, I want you to ask him something."

"And that is?"

"Ask him if he is into Satanism. Then call me back with what he said."

"Okay, I can do that."

Pat turned off the phone and jumped as she felt someone enter the room.

"I didn't mean to scare you. I heard the cell ring, so I got up to see what is going on."

"Yeah, it was Phil. It seems a man came into the station saying he has a male ghost threatening to kill everyone in the house unless he is made welcome into the home."

"Sounds like a real nut case. What the hell is wrong with Phil that he is not calling the nut house to come get the man?"

"I wondered the same thing. Phil feels that something is not right. I told him to ask the man if he is into Satanism and give me a call back about his answer."

"Can't wait to hear this," DK laughed as he walked over to sit on the couch.

All remained quiet before DK interrupted the silence.

"So what were you doing out here, looking out the window? Are you upset about something I can help you with?"

Without turning, she said quietly, "Not really. I was thinking about some things. Not anything you need to bother with."

"Believe me, Pat, anything that upsets you is no bother for me to get involved."

"If I tell you what I was thinking about, it would just start another fight, and I am not in the mood for that."

"You don't need to say what it's all about; then, it's about our getting married and not having kids. Am I close?"

She turned slightly to give him a sad glance, then returned to looking out the window.

"Pat, let's not get into all this right now. I already said I don't want to be a father, so that should be the end of it."

"All right. We should be hearing from

Phil shortly anyway."

Her words were barely spoken when her cell began to ring.

"I asked him if he is into Satanism, and he became very angry, saying he is a devout Christian."

"Okay, now the question is, do we come to the station or his home?"

"Might just as well come to his home. And, too, I have a question for you. If an evil entity does haunt his home, do you think we should call one of the priests and have them bring holy water?"

"Let me see what is going on first. No reason to have a priest up this early unless it is needed."

Pat writes down the man's address before getting to her feet.

"Guess it is time to go haunted house checking."

When DK pulled up in front of a large three-story blue house surrounded by wrought iron fencing, Pat sat quietly looking at the house.

DK remained silent, giving her time to try and see what she could find out before going inside.

When they saw Phil and two police cars pull up behind DK's vehicle, they stepped to the curb.

DK placed an arm around Pat's waist as they walked to the front door.

Phil waited for the man accompanying him to unlock the door, then stepped to the side to motion Pat and DK inside.

DK looks over at Phil and shakes his head.

Phil put a hand on the man's shoulder.

"Where do you want everyone to sit?"

"Right over here on the sofa," he directed

them into the front room, "I want you all to be comfortable."

"Phil, I am going to sit in this chair as I need to be alone."

"Everyone will need to stay quiet. Miss Lancaster is a psychic and will need silence while she sees what is going on here," Phil says.

"Thank you, Phil," Pat says. "Also, is anyone else in the house?"

"My wife and children are at my mother's house. After I was told by what is here and what we can expect, I did not want any of my family in this house."

Pat takes three deep breaths and closes her eyes.

The man seated on the couch with DK and Phil watches her.

"I was raised to believe that those professing to be psychic are from the devil."

"You were told wrong. Pat Lancaster is not evil; her gift comes from Our Holy Father." DK spoke up.

"I am simply saying what my parents and the preacher at my church told me." His voice took on a self protective tone.

"When someone is given a gift to help find people who are missing, find a killer and bring them to justice, help a soul who has recently left their body to find their way to the Holy Light, you can believe me when I tell you that does not come from Satan."

"Listening to you, I must admit I can almost believe in what you are saying."

"DK," Pat opens her eyes, "call a priest to come now and bring Holy Water."

DK pulls his cell forward and walks from the room.

Phil gets to his feet and sits beside the chair where Pat is seated.

"What are you finding, Pat? I am

beginning to get chills up and down my back."

"I don't doubt it. The entity in this house is filled with anger. While he is not evil, he can cause harm to others in his need to control."

"All right," DK said as he sat down on the couch. "Father Baldwin will be here shortly."

"Since I'm not Catholic, are you sure a priest can remove what is here?"

"Mr. Reems, Clergy Men do not pick and choose who they help. If someone is in trouble and needs their Godly help, they step forward and help," Phil says as he pulls his weapon from the holster.

DK glanced over at him and grinned.

"Phil, you don't need your gun. The son of a bitch is already dead."

"Yeah, I know, but I like to be prepared."

"There he is!" The words flew out of Reems' mouth, making them all turn to see where he was pointing.

Pat sits up straight in her chair. "I want all of you to step out of the house. I need to take care of this alone."

"I will be staying here, Pat," DK tells her before sitting near her chair.

Phil and Reems walk out the door.

"What is your name, and why are you threatening the Reems family?"

"My name is Steven Masterson, and I own this house."

"Steven, do you know you are dead and no longer the owner?"

"Yes, I am aware that I am dead."

"Why haven't you crossed over to the Other Side?"

"I need to stay and keep others from occupying my dwelling. Mr. Reems has been told to leave, or he and his family will suffer the consequences."

"All of your family are on the Other Side

and await your coming to be with them."

"You do not know this. You say this to get me to leave."

"Steven, I see a tall, slender woman in her early fifties wearing a light blue robe and nightgown. She says her name is Rhea and that she was your wife."

"How do you know this? Rhea was my wife and the mother of my five children."

"Rhea, will you come forward and speak with Steven?"

For a few moments, they remained alone. Then, a woman dressed in the robe and gown Pat described appears in the room.

"Steven, we have been waiting for you to come home and be with us. We love you and miss you. Take my hand, and let me lead you home."

Without hesitation, Steven reached out, taking the hand of the woman smiling at him.

As the two disappeared into the bright light surrounding them, Pat looked at DK.

"I guess this case is over."

DK reaches out a hand to pull Pat to her feet.

"Let's give Reems the good news and tell him to call the good father and tell him he need not make a trip."

"Too bad all our cases can't end this quickly and safely."

"I agree 100%." He pulled her against his hip as they approached their waiting vehicle.

CHAPTER ELEVEN

"I guess the time has come for us to get ahold of Phil and his wife and set up a time for us to get together with the Justice of the Peace to help us tie a firm knot and make Stormy and Ash proud of their mom and dad."

"We can do that. I don't think a discussion is needed on what needs to be done next. I love you, and you love me, so I feel we can be a strong married couple."

DK pulls Pat to her feet and into his arms to kiss her parted lips.

"You have no idea how happy you have just made me. I'll call Phil and ask him and his wife to join us for dinner tonight. Your choice of where we want to go."

"Our favorite restaurant, of course. I

think 7 pm. is a good time to have dinner."

"I think any time is a good time to eat. Now all we have to worry about is that none of us has an emergency to run to."

Pat laughed before turning away.

***

"I'm glad the two of you could join us. I know you are wondering why we invited you this evening."

Pat smiles at the couple seated across from them.

"I have a strong feeling it has to do with the two of you needing a Matron of Honor and a Best Man to stand with you while you both promise to love and honor one another."

The pretty woman dressed in a pair of black slacks and a white pullover top grins a wide grin.

"You could not be more right," DK speaks up, his eyes showing how pleased he is at her words.

"I always knew that you would finally get together sooner or later. And, of course, I was right." Phil laughed aloud.

"Far as I'm concerned, the way you are both dressed in neat-looking slacks and pullovers, we could stand before a preacher right now."

"Now, DK, I think you and your lovely wife-to-be will want your standups to be better attired than this," Phil tells him.

"My husband is so smart." Deb smiles.

"I have to agree, Deb," Pat says. "This will be a special day, and I want to thank the two of you for wanting to be a part of it."

"Phil, since you are such an important part of this town, you should know if there are any preachers who will not mind two beautiful German Shepherds attending the wedding?"

"I know a sure way you can be sure of their attending. Why don't the two of you get married at our house? We for sure would be happy to have them attend."

"I think that is a great idea, Deb," Phil says.

"DK, I am all for Deb's idea; what do you think?"

"Pat, as long as you are my wife, I couldn't care if we get married in Phil's office."

"Well, we don't want to go that far." Phil picks up the menu to begin scanning the culinary choices.

DK signals the waitress to come forward.

"Is everyone okay with a bottle of the restaurant's best champagne?"

"I will let you decide." Pat smiles.

After the champagne was poured, DK lifted his glass into the air.

"Here to a lasting friendship. Your willingness to be a part of making our dream come true will never be forgotten."

They each tapped a glass lightly before taking a sip of the aged wine.

***

With Stormy and Ash lying on the floor at their feet, Pat and DK relaxed beside each other on the couch.

"I have already taken a strong liking for Deb. She is so open-minded and outspoken, she reminds me a lot of Phil. But then, she would have to be understanding to be his wife."

"This is the first time I've met her. I do know Phil has a profound love for her. He can't mention her name without a broad grin spreading across his face."

"Exactly the way a healthy relationship should be. I have to say that now that we have finally decided to stop talking around our relationship and agreed to make it permanent, I feel a lot more anxious to be Mrs. Walker."

Without a word, DK reached over,

pulling her against him.

"I think we should go upstairs and begin practicing being Mr. and Mrs. Walker."

She allows him to pull her to her feet with an agreeable smile.

CHAPTER TWELVE

Pat poured the morning coffee as DK pulled a chair away from the table and sat down.

"I don't know about you, but I had a very restful night's sleep. We should always make it a point to work out before going to sleep."

DK looked at her with a grin. "I think you're right, my beautiful fiancé."

"I love the sounds of that. However, I have to say I will like the name I am about to receive soon."

"And that is?"

"I will be known as Mrs. DK Walker."

"You will not enjoy being called Mrs. DK Walker any more than I will love introducing you as Mrs. DK Walker."

Pat looked over at him. Her face showed sadness.

"I wish we hadn't quarreled over being married."

"My darling, we can't go back; we can only move forward, and as the old saying goes, all's well that ends well. And trust me, this is the start of a great relationship."

Pat laughed, "It already is. We proved this last night."

"Again," DK added.

The ringing of her cell phone on the table made DK shake his head.

"Hello, Phil, Pat said, bringing the phone to her ear.

"Time to go to work. Just had a call about a missing teenager named Ronnie. Guess he was with some friends at the skating rink and never showed when he was supposed to be home. The parents called the boy's friends, and they all said his dad had come to the rink and picked him up."

"If his dad picked him up, why are the parents calling the friends about the no-show? Unless the dad who picked him up is the boy's biological dad, and he has a stepdad."

"Yeah, the boy's parents were divorced, and he has a stepdad. The thing is, according to the boy's mother, the boy's dad is deceased."

"Let me get this straight. The friends all said the boy's dad was the one who picked him up. So, do the friends know the boy's dad, and are they sure this is the person who picked the boy up from the rink?"

"The boy's friends say they have known the entire Roberts family for years, as they all used to live in the same neighborhood. And they all attended the dad's funeral."

"I take it we are all going to the boy's parents' house?"

"Yes, they are expecting us. The address is 146 Aulbary Street. I don't mind telling you

I find this more than a tad strange."

"I agree. DK and I will meet you at the boy's parents' house within the hour."

Pat hung up the call and laid the phone on the table.

"I take it we are going to work. So what are we battling this time?"

Pat filled DK in on what was happening as he opened the back door to let Stormy and Ash outside.

As both the dogs ran in different directions, DK laughed.

"I think we let them outside to do their business just in time."

***

DK pulled before a three-story white house and shut off the motor.

"Looks like Phil hasn't made it here yet. We should wait for him before we go to the door."

"I am sure this is what he would want. We know it isn't always easy to introduce a psychic."

"Yes, and compound that with a man who is supposed to be dead picking up his son."

At that moment, they see Phil turn into the driveway.

DK opened his car door to step onto the street.

"Looks like we made it at the same time. You can follow me up to the front door."

A woman who looked to be in her early forties and dressed in a pair of brown slacks and a lighter brown blouse met them at the door.

"Thank you all for coming." She stepped to the side to allow them to enter.

A man who looked to be in the same age group and dressed in blue jeans and a white T-shirt directed them to be seated on a white leather couch in the living room. His overly sad appearance had Pat and DK sharing a brief glance.

When everyone was seated, Phil introduced the couple to Pat, DK, and himself.

"I have brought along two people who work with the different police precincts to solve the most difficult cases. Pat Lancaster is a psychic. DK Walker is a police officer."

The woman shook her head, saying briefly, "We need the help of the police, not a witch."

"Pat Lancaster is not a witch, Madam. Now, do you want our help or not? If you do, I will need you to bring something your son has used, a hairbrush with the hair still in the brush, or a toothbrush. We will wish you a good day if you do not want our help.

For a long moment, she remained silent, then, throwing up her hands, she told the man beside her to go upstairs and bring them

Ronnie's hairbrush.

"If you don't mind, Mrs. Waters, I will sit over here in this lovely chair and conduct my business," Pat says.

"No, that's fine. My name is Sarah. I want to get on with finding my son."

"This is why we are here," Phil speaks up, taking the hairbrush handed to him.

"I didn't get your name," Phil says, looking up at the man staring at him.

"My name is Russel."

"Thank you, Russel," Pat tells him, taking the hairbrush from Phil. I know not everyone finds it easy to accept help from a source you have most likely been taught is evil. Trust me, most psychics have been given their gift from God."

"If we could get on with getting on, my wife and I would appreciate it."

"Phil," Pat says, holding up a hand, "it's

alright."

Pat holds the hairbrush in her hand and takes three deep breaths. Within moments, she sees a tall, handsome man dressed in a military outfit. He acknowledges her and steps forward to stand beside the chair she is seated in.

"My name is Paul Roberts. I did not mean for my son's friends to see me when I came to speak with Ronnie. Ronnie can see me since he, like you, is psychic. My son Ronnie is in grave danger. You will find him in the home of his grandparents. Ronnie asked them to protect him."

"Protect him from whom?"

"From his stepfather, Russel. Russel is jealous of Ronnie. He is angry that Sarah bore me a son, yet has been unable to have more children."

"Thank you for your warning, Paul. I will see what I can do to protect your son from

Russel's anger."

Paul stepped back further into the room.

Pat opened her eyes and remained silent for a few minutes.

"What have you been able to find out, Pat?" Phil asked.

"Sarah, how has Ronnie been treated since you and Russel have been together?"

"Ronnie and Russel do not get along."

"Why do you think this is?"

"Ronnie has been angry since I divorced his father. I admit it was wrong of me to have an affair while still married, but I fell in love with Russel. I divorced Paul so Russel and I could be together. Ronnie resents this. Ronnie became even more resentful of Russel when Paul contracted cancer and died."

"Russel, how do you feel about Ronnie being Sarah's only child and her being unable to give you a child?"

"What in the hell does all this have to do with his being missing? I thought psychics were supposed to be able to see what the hell is going on."

"Russel, please. I want to find my son."

"Oh, by all means, Russel, shut the hell up so we can concentrate on little Ronnie!"

"You don't like Ronnie, do you, Russel?" DK spoke up.

"I don't have any problem with him as long as he stays the hell out of my way."

"I think it goes much deeper than that, Russel. I think you would be glad if you never had to lay eyes on him again."

"You stupid bitch! I just said, as long as he stays out of my way, everything can be fine!"

"But wouldn't it be better if Ronnie had never been? If he was completely out of your and Sarah's life?"

"You're turning my words! I didn't say I wish he were dead!"

"But that's how I think you really feel about my son," Sarah whispered.

"You can shut the hell up, you stupid bitch! If you want the truth, I wish both you and that little bastard you gave birth to were dead. And maybe I'll see what I can do to make that happen!"

DK jumped as Russel drew back his hand to accost Sarah.

"You just signed your arrest warrant, you jealous sonofabitch!" DK told him as he flipped him around to lock his hands in cuffs.

"You have been abused all your married life with Russel. Am I right, Sarah?"

"I never knew what a terrible and cruel man he could be to me and Ronnie."

"I will need you to press charges on Russel, Sarah. He will be going to jail."

"You press charges on me, bitch. I will see you and that little sonofabitch you call your son dead."

"I will let Ronnie know it is safe for him to come home," Phil said.

"You have found him?" Sarah's hand went to her throat.

"Ronnie has been with his grandparents. You may want to know and plan how you will deal with Ronnie being psychic. This is how Ronnie could see him when he came to warn him of the danger awaiting him. It was only by accident that his friends could see his dad, too," Pat told her.

"Thank you all so much for your help."

"You are very welcome, Sarah," Phil told her as he shoved Russel ahead of him.

"Time to call it a day." DK grinned as he placed a loving arm over Pat's shoulders.

CHAPTER THIRTEEN

"Deb wants to know if we want to send out invitations to our wedding before we set a date."

"I don't want to put off our wedding for weeks. I want to get married now. We still need to find a preacher."

"Phil and Deb have taken care of that need, too. They talked with the preacher at the Lutheran Church they attend, and he is willing to marry us. So, now all we need to do is set a date and get the knot tied."

"Do you want to find outfits for the children? I think it would be cute to dress them up."

"We can do that. I don't know how comfortable they would be with a tux and a dress. Guess we can find out."

"I hope you don't want me to wear a tux. That is not going to happen."

"I am not going to wear a wedding gown, either. We can go into town and find a nice suit for you and a nice suit for me."

"I haven't been this excited in years. How about we finish our coffee and go into town? Then, when we find the outfits we will wear, we can call Deb and set everything up for this Saturday."

Pat picks up her cup of coffee and gets to her feet to walk over to the sink to dump the coffee.

"Do you want me to dump yours, too?"

"Without a word, DK hands her his cup.

"I think we need to get the kids ready to go along. They may need to be measured to be sure their outfits will fit."

***

Pat and DK could not believe all the people standing on the beautiful, well-decorated green lawn.

"I thought I said we did not know anyone to invite. We may have forgotten them, but they sure have not forgotten us."

"I am glad so many showed up," Pat said. "It looks like Phil and Deb invited half the town."

A preacher dressed in a long white robe and carrying a thick Bible walked to stand in the middle of the lawn. He motioned the couple to step forward.

"I guess there is no turning back now," DK leaned to the side to whisper.

"If you wish, I can tell the preacher we have changed our minds."

"You do, and they will see the wedding conducted with you over my shoulder."

They all laughed as Storm and Ash approached them. Storm is dressed in a dress, and Ash is dressed in a suit, their tails wagging to stand beside them.

The pastor opened his Bible to begin the ceremony. When he finished reading, he said the words, making them man and wife.

DK drew Pat into his arms to kiss her full mouth delightedly.

Amid all the hugs and congratulatory kisses, they walked into the house, where a beautiful wedding cake awaited them on the dining room table.

Deb handed a knife to Pat.

"You can cut the cake now. After you and DK have shared the first piece, I will cut the rest of the cake and serve your guests."

***

Pat turned over in the bed and drew one hand down the side of DK's face.

"I don't know about you, but our lovemaking as Mr. and Mrs. Walker tonight felt no different than all the other times I have enjoyed making love with you."

DK pulled her hand forward, kissing the center of her palm.

"I have always felt we belong together. However, I am glad you belong to me in every way."

Pat pushed her body against him, and when she felt his arms surrounding her, she closed her eyes and drifted off to sleep, only to come back to the present with the ringing of her cell phone.

"Damn it to hell! A man can't even have a peaceful wedding night."

Pat picks up the phone and turns off the ringer.

"Hello."

"Sorry to intrude on your special night, Pat, but we just got a call about a killer on the loose in my neighborhood, of all places," Phil said.

"Where exactly are we talking about?"

"Would you believe four houses down from ours?"

"Do you want us to meet you at your house or just go on to the house where the attack occurred? I am sure deputies are already there."

"No, as a matter of fact, they aren't. I know the neighbor; his name is Pete Jenkins, and the one who was attacked is his wife, Jenny. Meet me here, and I'll take you to the house."

"All right. We'll see you in about forty-five minutes."

"I'll go let the babies out," DK said, getting to his feet. "On the way out, I'll turn on the coffee."

"I wish we had time to take a shower."

"Why don't we? Phil can wait. From what I was able to glean on the speaker, the person who was attacked isn't going anywhere."

"Okay, let the babies outside, and we can shower quickly."

***

Phil was backing out of his driveway as they drove up.

"If a murder were to occur in our neighborhood, you would be right beside me if I had to leave the house. I don't care how many locks are on the doors."

"I'm sure Phil told her to keep the doors locked."

They drove up in front of a light tan two-story house.

As they exited their vehicles, a tall man dressed in pajamas and a robe ran out of the house.

"Hurry up!" he shouted. "I think she is still alive."

Phil keyed his cell, requesting an ambulance.

"All right, an ambulance will be here shortly."

Phil turned the man around and walked with him to the front door.

"You need to show me where Jenny is, Pete."

"Yes, come on, she is in the guest room upstairs. We had a little spat earlier, and she slept in the other room."

They raced upstairs and into the guest room.

They saw a small woman nude from the waist down, lying on the floor beside the bed.

Phil quickly checked her pulse and was glad when he found she was still alive.

"Jenny, can you hear me?" Phil said.

"Keep him away from me. Oh, God, keep him away from me," Jenny cried.

"You're safe, Jenny. No one is going to hurt you. Can you tell me who attacked you?"

"Yes. It was Jason Bagel next door. He climbed into the bedroom window. He hit me in the face before I could scream for Pete."

"That sonofabitch!" Pete growled. "I'll kill him!"

"You just stay right here," Phil told him, reaching out to keep him in the room.

"Who are those two?" Pete gestured to Pat and DK.

"They work for the police department. When you told me what happened, I thought Jenny had been murdered. Pat here is a psychic, and I thought she could help find the one who had hurt Jenny."

"Maybe I still can," Pat spoke up. "I can try and find out why the man who attacked Jenny did what he did."

At the sounds of pounding on the front door, DK ran downstairs to usher in the Ambulance Crew.

When Jenny was ready for transport,

Pete leaned over to place a tender kiss on the side of her face.

"I am coming with you, Sweetheart. Phil and the ones he has brought with him can stay here and see what they can find out."

Jenny nodded as she clutched his hand.

"You can lock up when you're ready to leave. I don't doubt that the man Jenny said attacked her is Jason, but I know that before you call in deputies to arrest him, you will want to be sure you have the right man. I'll be with Jenny at the hospital when you are ready to talk with us."

Pat sat down on the side of the bed and breathed deeply, relaxing her mind.

A short, stocky man with balding hair who looked in his late sixties and dressed in jeans and a light tan pullover entered her mind. She watched him pad over to look down at Jenny. He drew back a balled fist and hit Jenny in the side of the face. Wasting no time, he yanked her onto the floor and proceeded to rape her. When he finished, he stood up, pulled his jeans on, and looked down at her. In a quiet voice, Pat heard him whisper. "I thought it only fair that since your husband enjoys having sex with my wife, I should be able to enjoy sex on his wife." With that said, he turned and climbed back out the bedroom window.

Pat opened her eyes and sat there momentarily, shaking her head.

"I take it from your actions now that you learned what happened and why," DK said.

"Oh yes, I learned why this happened."

"What were you able to find out, Pat?" Phil walked over to stand before her.

"Seems old Pete has been having an affair with Jason's wife. In Jason's mind, this gave him the right to have sex with Pete's wife."

"Guess we can go next door with a few deputies and arrest Jason. This should break up two couples."

"Life can be a real bitch at times," DK murmured as Phil keyed his cell to call the station and have them send out two deputies.

"I guess we can go home and go back to bed," Pat laughed, placing her arm around DK's waist as they walked out of the room.

CHAPTER FOURTEEN

Pat opened her car door to step into the garage when her cell began to ring.

Well fuck me runnin'," DK growled. "Can't Phil wait until tomorrow to tell us what old Jason had to say on his behalf?"

"Hello."

"Hello, Pat. Sorry to wake you. This is Detective Roberts of the Reasor Police Department."

"I wasn't asleep, Detective. I just got home from solving a case for Phil Abbot. What do you need?"

"We just had a murder reported. A man and his wife were shot over on 360 Sennet Street. Can you meet me and my detectives there in half an hour?"

"Yes, we will be there," She told him before turning off the cell.

"I take it our going back to bed is not going to happen for a few hours."

"Yes, we need to meet Detective Roberts to see what I can find out about a murder. We should check on the kids before we take off again."

"I'll go see to them. We should have some coffee left in the pot, so I'll pour some to take with us."

"I don't know what I would do without you, my love."

"You will never have to worry your pretty little head about that."

***

"Nice looking house," Pat said as DK pulled up behind a red Buick Saber.

The house in question was a three-story green with white trim.

DK stepped to the curb to walk around the vehicle and open Pat's car door.

Roberts walked up to them and stuck out a hand.

"Glad you could get here so promptly."

"Lead off, Detective," DK told him. "The sooner we get through here, the sooner we can all go home."

"Yeah," he glanced at his watch, "being out and about at almost 2 am is a pain."

"And we all know where that pain resides," DK laughed.

"How did you learn about this murder, Detective?" Pat asked him.

"A neighbor heard the gunshots and called the station. He said something was always going on with the people living in the house."

"If this is so, then maybe we are investigating a suicide instead of a double murder."

"Could be, Pat. These days, anything is possible.

A young deputy met them as they walked through the front door.

"Both bodies are in the Master Bedroom upstairs."

As they walked into the bedroom, they saw a man who looked to be in his early fifties and a woman about the same age. They were both nude, and both had a gunshot to the temple.

"I'll need to have it quiet while I find out what happened here."

She relaxed her mind and body, allowing the images to come forth. She saw a short, fat man in his late seventies wearing a pair of black slacks and a woman's blue blouse. He had a mop of white hair, and his entire mouth was painted with red lipstick. He walked into the Master Bedroom. His unhurried steps claimed his ease in being in someone else's house. She watched him stand by the queen-size bed filled with the couple in question and saw him begin to laugh. He pulled a pistol from the leather holster and fired off two shots into the temple of the man and woman on the bed. She watched him, hoping he would speak and say why he did what he did. Finally, he voiced the words she needed to hear.

"I am a woman, and you cannot change this. Your laughter at my expense and the expense of my husband will no longer fill you with the glee you feel when in our presence."

Pat watched the killer turn and walk out of the room and down the stairs. He stepped outside and climbed into a pink pickup. She quickly zeroed in on the license plate.

She opened her eyes and turned to DK as he sat in a chair near the bed.

"Write down this license plate number. It is on a pink Chevy pickup belonging to the killer."

"This should let Roberts find the one who committed these murders," DK said. "I take it there was only one killer involved in the shooting?"

"Yes, he acted alone. I guess he was living out his revenge on the couple because they made fun of him being a transgender person."

Since this murder is recent, Roberts should be able to get a line on the owner of a pink pickup. I don't think too many men drive a pink pickup since trucks are considered macho."

"Or so rumor has it," Pat replied.

"Were you able to find out if we are dealing with a suicide or a murder?" Roberts stood up from the chair he had been occupying.

"It is a murder. I got the license plate number on the pink pickup the killer is driving.

"That is excellent news. I always thought you were a pro. Thank you, Pat. Be sure to stop by the station later today for a well-deserved check."

"You can count on it, Detective Roberts, Pat told him as DK handed him the paper with the license plate number. "For now, we will wish you a good night."

"Let's get home and relax before another sicko lives out a need to act out a revengeful act."

***

Settled into the large bed, DK pulls Pat's body close against him.

"I can't believe I am saying this, but I am too tired to carry this further."

"I could pretend you are the only one who feels this way, but I can't. Goodnight and pleasant dreams."

"Right back at you, Mrs. Walker. Right back at you."

CHAPTER FIFTEEN

"I am ready for a stack of pancakes, three over easy eggs, strips of crisp bacon, and strong cups of coffee. Now, am I going to try and fix this myself, only to take a chance of being interrupted by an officer of the law who needs my expertise, or go to a restaurant and allow them to fix it for us?"

Although you are an excellent cook and always set the tastiest food before me, I vote we go out to eat and have our stomachs full before heading out on another case. We know that phone will ring, so why waste time?"

"I agree. Also, since it is a lovely day out, let's take the kids with us. They love to go bye-bye."

"I think that is a right good idea."

***

Pat pushed her plate away and smiled.

"Now, that was an excellent breakfast."

"Let's hope now we don't get called to a murder that is so out there we lose it all."

"You keep talking like that, and I won't need to wait on a new sickening case. I'll lose it before we walk out the door here."

"Sorry."

Pat started to get to her feet when her cell began to ring.

"Here we go," DK said.

"Hello, Detective Roberts. I hope all is still well."

"Everything could not be better. "The sicko in the pink pickup is now in custody here at the station. I knew the two of you would want to know we got him. So, I guess I'll see you when you stop by to pick up your check."

"Yes, we just finished breakfast and will

stop by in a few minutes. See you then."

"That, as you heard, was Roberts telling me they got the killer, and he is already in custody at the station."

"Now, that is what I like to hear. It just goes to prove that a ringing on your cell is not always invasive."

At that moment, Pat's cell rings as though to prove him wrong.

"Hello, yes, this is Pat Lancaster."

"Hello Pat. This is Sheldon Meadows. I am a principal of Lane High School. I understand you are a Psychic?"

"That is correct, Mr. Meadows. How can I help you?"

"One of our students here has been telling her class that a male ghost is haunting her."

"Would you say this student has a low IQ and is failing most of her grades?"

"On the contrary. She is a straight-A

student. This is why her teachers have brought this to my attention."

"Have you or any of her teachers spoken with the girl's parents?"

"Yes, Miss Willis, her biology teacher, has spoken with the girl's mother. According to Miss Willis, the mother agrees that a male ghost is haunting her daughter."

"What is the girl's name, and what do you want to do about this concerning me?"

"The girl's name is Cindy. Would you be willing to go with me to the girl's home and speak with her parents? I am willing to pay you. When speaking with Phil Abbot, I was given your name, your ability as a psychic, and what you earn by doing what you do."

"Yes, I can go with you. When do you want to go? I will accompany DK Walker, who also works for Phil Abbot."

"That's fine. Would this evening at 6 pm be all right?"

"Yes."

She lives at 608 Persion Ave. Until then, Pat."

"Guess we have a haunting to investigate this evening at 6 PM."

"Hauntings are always interesting," DK says.

"Some are even more. Some can be downright evil."

"The good thing is the evil ones can be sent back to hell. You taught me that."

"All ghosts can be sent away. And they need to be sent away. They need to go home and be surrounded by the Holy Light. The ones being sent back to hell is a different matter."

"One thing I keep asking myself about the cases I have been with you on is how in the hell you can put up with all you are involved with?"

"Father gave me a gift, and I use my gift to

help others. I don't question the Holy Father."

The man who answered their knock was tall, with a full head of black hair, blue eyes, and dressed in blue jeans and a brown short-sleeved shirt.

"Hello, Pat and DK," he held out a hand to each of them. "Please come in."

"Thank you, Pat says."

"All right, you are both here," A short, stocky man in his late fifties comes forth. "I am pleased to meet you both. I am Sheldon Meadows. This gentleman is Randy Buchanan, and his wife, Sylvia. Thank you for coming." He shakes both their hands.

A very attractive blond woman in her early forties, green-eyed and wearing an ankle-length blue dress and high-heeled blue shoes, steps forward. "Thank you for coming to help us find out what is threatening our daughter, Cindy."

"We are always glad to help," Pat tells

her.

"Now, the way I work is to sit quietly and see what comes into my mind's eye."

She and DK are directed to be seated in two white leather chairs.

After breathing deeply, Pat closes her eyes.

For a few moments, all is silent with no one in view; then, a spiritual form begins to take shape. The male standing in view is no more than late teens with black hair, green eyes, and very handsome. She sees him enter the bedroom of the young girl being haunted, to stand looking down at her. Then he kisses the tips of his fingers and reaches out, placing them on her forehead as she sleeps. He turns and walks out of the room.

Pat opens her eyes and sits up straighter in her chair.

"How long have you lived in this house, and are you renting or buying?"

The woman sitting on the couch speaks up. "We are the owners of this house. It has been a little over four years since we bought this house."

"Were you acquainted with the former owners?"

"Not really. We met them when we came to look at the house," Sheldon says.

"Did they have any children? If so, what were their ages?"

The Real Estate Agent who showed us the house, Brad Rollins, said they were selling the house because their teenage son, Steven, was killed in an auto accident some months earlier."

"What is the name of the people you bought this house from?"

"James and Patty Davis. Why are you asking about them?"

"I am asking about them, Randy, because the ghost of a young man looks to be a teenager."

"So, what you are saying is, the former owners of this house sold the house because their teenage son was killed?"

"Let me check out something before I answer your question."

Pat again closed her eyes and relaxed her mind. Once again, she brings the young man forth.

"Are you Steven, the young man who once lived here?"

"Yes. I don't mean any harm to Cindy. She is so pretty, and I am so lonely. I just want her to be a friend to me."

"Steven, you are aware that you are no longer alive? You were killed in an auto accident."

"Yes, I know this."

"Instead of frightening Cindy, you should let me send you home to the other side where your loved ones who have gone before you are waiting."

"If you think this is what I should do, you can send me home. My grandparents are in heaven, and I would love to be with them again. They always gave me so much love."

"Look around until you see a bright light and a path leading to a golden gate. Walk up that path and enter into the Heavenly Kingdom."

"Yes, I see the bright light and the path. Thank you for helping me," he tells Pat before walking up the path and through the gate.

Pat opens her eyes and looks around the room.

"Steven is no longer here. He has gone home to the other side where his loved ones wait to greet him."

Sylvia gets to her feet and puts her arms around Pat in a tight hug.

"Thank you for your help. I will write

you a check for your services."

"Don't bother. We will chalk this up to helping two teens."

DK gets up from his chair to place a hand on Pat's shoulder.

"I guess we can head home."

"I am right behind you."

CHAPTER SIXTEEN

As Pat opens the car door, her cell tells her she is needed.

"I am going to go let the kids out in the backyard," DK says.

"Yeah, I'll let you know what's up, if anything."

"Hi, Pat. Phil here."

"Hi, Phil. What do you need at this time?"

"Got a murder. An entire family, except for the husband, is dead."

"Where was the husband when the murders occurred?"

"Says he was grocery shopping. According to him, his wife has the flu, so he has to do everything alone."

How many bodies?"

"Five kids and the wife."

"How long before you meet us at the address?"

"I am staring over there as soon as we hang up. Name's Rick Blanchard at 872 Wyoming Boulevard. That would make it about three blocks from you and DK."

"Let me have a cup of coffee and relax, then we can come over there. I just got home from a case involving a haunting."

"Just what you need, another case to solve."

"This is my job. See you in a few."

Pat ends their chat and gets to her feet to go outside and tell DK what they will be involved in.

"I so wish we could simply spend the day playing with these two entertaining individuals," he gestures to the two German

Shepherds, trying to get his attention, but from the look on your face, I can already see that is not going to happen."

"Phil just informed me there was a murder about three blocks from here. An entire family. The husband is the only one who was not involved."

"The only one not murdered, you mean. We have no idea if he may have been involved."

"Let's go enjoy a cup of coffee, then we can go see what we can see."

***

DK drove down the street, looking for the address Pat said is the crime scene.

"Yeah, there it is on the left, the two-story brown house."

"I don't see Phil's car here, so I guess we will sit here until he arrives."

"You said an entire family was murdered. How the hell can anyone murder an entire family?"

"It takes a sick mind, this is for sure."

"Okay, Phil just turned onto this street."

"I wish he would bring some deputies to the crime scenes. I keep urging him to do this, but he keeps ignoring me."

"Maybe he feels that I am enough."

"You could be right. Let's go see what we are in for this time," Pat says, getting out of the vehicle.

"I hope the husband is home so I don't have to kick in the door," Phil told them.

"If it comes to that, I'll do the kicking."

"You think this old man can't get it done, is that it?"

"You said it, I didn't." DK laughs, slapping him on the back.

"Okay, you two. We're at a murder scene. Try to act your age."

"Okay, Mom, we'll give it our best shot." Phil grins.

A slim man in his early thirties with blond hair, dressed in jeans and a T-shirt, comes to the door as they move up the sidewalk.

"Hello," Phil holds out a hand. "I am Detective Abbott, and this is Pat Lancaster Walker and her husband, DK Walker."

"I am glad to meet you," he shook Phil's hand and held out his other hand to DK.

"What can you tell me about what went on here?"

"I came home from shopping and found my wife and kids lying on the living room carpet. I could see they had been shot. I don't know how I am going to live with this." His voice cracked as he swiped a hand over his eyes.

"Pat, do you want to hear more before you view the bodies?"

"Are you a policewoman, Pat?"

"I am a psychic. I work with the different police precincts to help them solve their most difficult cases."

"And your husband comes with you in case you run into any danger."

"Trust me, my wife can handle what she comes up against just fine."

Phil put a hand on DK's shoulder.

"Why don't the three of us go into the kitchen and sit at the table while Pat sees what she can find out?"

"Thank you, Phil. I will sit down in the chair beside the end table."

"Yes," Rick tells her, "that chair is very comfortable."

Pat inhales deep breaths through her nasal passages, holding the breaths before releasing them through the mouth. When her mind and body are relaxed, she sits quietly to see what or who will come forth.

She sees a short, fat, bald man, except for the tuffs of white hair on the sides of his head, who looks to be in his late sixties, in black slacks and a black suit coat covering a white shirt. He smiles at the three girls and two boys lying on the floor watching TV. A tall, brown-haired woman in her early thirties wearing a yellow dress comes into the room and tells the children to prepare for dinner.

The man reaches into his jacket pocket to pull out a pistol and, aiming the gun at the woman, pulls the trigger. The room is filled with screams from the watching children until, one by one, the weapon silences their screams. The man turns without a backward glance and walks out of the room.

Pat opens her eyes and gets to her feet.

DK looks up as Pat comes into the kitchen.

"Were you able to find out who did this terrible tragedy?" DK speaks up.

"Yes. I was able to see the killer. We need

to get to the station and start going through mug shots. I hate to say this, but this is one evil individual who, unless stopped and stopped now, can become a serial killer."

"He may already be a serial killer, but in another state and town. Another thing we can get done is to get an artist's sketch out on TV and the paper. The more he is seen around town, the chances are he can be identified."

"We need to call the coroner and get the house taped off. We don't need anyone coming in and destroying evidence." DK says.

"Yeah, I am going to get on that right now," Phil says, bringing forth his cell.

***

Pat sits in front of the man, getting ready to sketch the killer Pat will describe for him.

"Ready when you are." He tells her.

"Let me get another look at his face. We can't afford any mistakes."

Taking the needed deep breaths to relax her mind, she brings forth the face of the killer. She watches him turn to leave the room and notices he has a pronounced limp. She opens her eyes and describes the man they need to find.

When the artist is finished, he turns the drawing around to show Pat.

"Does this look anything like the one the police need to find?"

"Yes. When a sketch is done, it often doesn't look like the described individual. You are a very talented artist, my friend."

"Thank you. I do my best."

***

Seated in an Italian Restaurant enjoying a meal, DK lays down his fork and looks across the table.

"The more you and I go on the different cases demanded of you, the more I feel guilty for all the times I tried to talk you out of continuing to do what you do for the police."

"You are seeing more now than you did before."

"Yes, but..."

"No, DK, we don't need to go into past anger and..." Pat stares across the room and pushes her plate across the table.

"What's wrong? You look like you're ready to ask for my gun."

"The sick sonofabitch who killed that family is seated four tables down from us."

"Are you sure?" DK pulls his gun from the holster hidden beneath his jacket.

"Yes, I am sure. There's no way I could forget that evil face."

DK pushes back his chair and gets to his feet.

"You wait here and call for backup. I am going to take him outside to protect the people in this restaurant."

DK slowly walks the short way to where the man is seated with a woman and two teens. Placing a firm hand beneath the man's elbow, he pulls upward.

"You need to come with me. I don't think you want to draw attention to your family, so don't make this difficult."

The man pushes back his chair and gets to his feet.

"I'll be back as soon as I find out what this is about," he tells those seated at the table. He reached into the small pocket of his short-sleeved shirt to draw forth some folded bills to lay them on the table.

Pat told the waitress who came up to the table to leave the food, that they would be back in a few minutes to finish their meal.

DK pushed the man in custody to his and Pat's vehicle.

"You are under arrest for the murder of an entire family."

"You have the wrong man, Officer. I have no idea when this murder occurred, but I can assure you I am not the one you are after."

"You don't want to say anymore," DK told him before giving him his Miranda rights.

A police car pulled up, and two officers stepped out.

"You need to take this man to the station. He is under arrest for murder."

One of the officers turned the man around and cuffed him before putting him in the police car.

"Let's go back inside and finish our meal."

***

Sitting on the couch, enjoying a much-needed drink, Pat smiled at DK.

"That was a fast turnaround. It's a good thing we were hungry for some good Italian food. However, I strongly believe that things happen for a reason."

She leans forward as her cell begins to ring.

"Hello, Phil. Are you calling to tell us we are two fast case solvers?" She laughed.

"No. I am calling to tell you you have the wrong man arrested for murder."

"I don't understand. I could not have been wrong about the man that I saw at the murder scene and now at the Restaurant."

DK looks at her, his face covered with astonishment

"While I am not surprised that you recognized the man you saw at the crime scene as the man in the restaurant, I am surprised that you did not get a psychic heads up that you have the wrong man."

"You need to explain what you are talking about, Phil." Her voice is taking on a tone of anger.

"The man brought to the station is not the killer. His twin brother is. The man arrested was happy to tell us where we could pick up his brother. He told us the rest of the family has little to do with him, as he has been in trouble all his life. Killing small animals and assaulting women. I have to say, when I saw the real killer, I was stunned. That is how much they look alike."

"I guess all we can say now is that all's well that ends well."

"I will toast to that." She lifts her glass into the air.

"Good night to you, Phil."

"Good night to you and DK."

CHAPTER SEVENTEEN

DK stretches his long legs out straight and heaves a sigh of contentment.

"You sound like a very contented man, DK," Pat tells him, setting a cup of coffee on the coffee table in front of him.

"You heard right, my love. If I were any more contented, I wouldn't be able to live with myself."

"I hope you are hungry. I am going to make us some pancakes, and bacon and eggs."

"I would not turn down anything you make, as you are by far the best cook in the world."

"I am going to leave my cell here on the coffee table. If I get a call, you can find out what is happening and tell them we are about to have breakfast, so whatever they need can wait."

"Oh!" He laughs and sits up straight. "Do I like the sounds of that!"

"So do I," she laughed before walking into the kitchen.

DK turned on the TV to watch the news. The face of a beautiful young black woman flashed on the screen with the caption, HAVE YOU SEEN THIS WOMAN? He continues to watch the screen to learn more about the missing woman. She is slender, with curly black hair and green eyes, and she is twenty-eight years old.

"Pat," DK calls out, "I think you need to come see this."

"Damn it, DK, I said whatever comes up can wait. I am fixing breakfast."

"This is important, Pat. You need to come here."

Pat walks into the living room with an

angry look on her face.

DK points to the TV. "This just came on the air."

Pat looks at the woman on the screen.

"You're right. This does need my attention."

"While you do what you do, I'll work on our meal." DK gets to his feet and walks into the kitchen.

Pat takes a few deep breaths before closing her eyes. She sees the woman on the screen talking with a young white male in his early teens.

"You should not be here, Danny. There is too much danger. Drug dealers and hookers live on this street. They are black. You are a white teenager. Leave while you still can."

"I want you to come with me, Lena. You are in danger, too."

"Danny, I know how much you hate the

fact that I am a prostitute, but the fact remains, I am. Now, stop being a pain in the ass and go home."

"Lena. Why in the hell are you wasting time? I expect you to make money, not stand around talking with a snot-nosed punk who can't even afford your services. Now get your ass to work or expect a severe beating."

The man standing beside her is in his late sixties, very obese, black with gray hair, and a large nose that has been broken more than once.

"I make more money than any of the other girls, so you don't need to run your mouth with threats, Earl."

"You mouth off to me one more time; my sharp-bladed knife is going to rip you up so bad won't no man want to lay you."

"Don't you dare touch her, you fat son of a bitch!" Danny steps forward.

Guess what, Lena? You just signed this

little bastard's death warrant."

"NO!" Lena cried, grabbing Danny's arm and slinging him away from the man, reaching into his pocket to bring forth a huge knife.

"Before Danny can move away, his chest is filled with the knife, and he falls forward onto the ground.

Lena rushed to Danny's side to drop to her knees beside him.

"You evil son of a bitch! You didn't have to do that! He was only a boy."

"I told him to shut up, but he wanted to play badass, so he only had himself to blame."

Lena withdrew a cell phone from the pocket of her slacks.

"What the hell do you think you're doin'?"

"I am calling an ambulance."

"Don't bother. When I take someone out, I do the job right the first time. He's dead, so he don't need no ambulance."

Lena placed two fingers on the side of Danny's throat. Feeling no pulse, she got to her feet.

"I suppose you expect me to go on like nothing has happened."

"Unless you want to join him, I suggest you get on with what you've been hired to do."

"You are one sick bastard. I am leavin'. I can't stomach lookin' at your ugly face anymore."

Laughing outright, Earl lunges forward and plunges the knife into Lena's chest.

The stark horror on her face brings a new burst of laughter into the silence.

"Guess some have to learn the hard way."

Motioning two tall black men forth, he pointed to both bodies on the street's side.

"Get these two hauled off and buried in

the woods. Hated to waste the best whore in my business, but no one disrespects me."

Pat opened her eyes and picked up her cell. When she heard Phil's voice on the other line, she told him what she had learned about the missing woman shown on the TV.

"Breakfast is done. So I guess after we've eaten, we will be joining Phil on the street to find the pimp who committed the murders."

***

Standing on the street talking with Phil, DK told him of his idea to bring the pimp out into the open.

"I am going to walk up the street alone. With any luck, one of the girls will show up to proposition me, and I can maybe get her to tell me the name of her pimp."

"Since we already know his first name is Earl, just ask her his last name and where you can find him. Tell her you have two good-looking girls in their late teens you want him to hire."

That should work. Okay, I'll catch you later."

"Good luck," Phil says before walking away.

Pat and Phil sit in Phil's jeep, watching DK as a young woman in her early twenties dressed in a provocative short black skirt and sheer light green top approaches him. Pat inhales an angry breath as the woman runs a hand up DK's arm.

"Keep it inside, Pat, keep it inside. She is a means to the end."

DK rubs the top of his head, the signal he knows where they can find the pimp, and with a wave of his hand, he walks towards Phil's jeep.

Phil starts the jeep as DK slides inside and shuts the door.

"He's living in an apartment right down the street. The hooker warned me to be extra careful, as old Earl has a very volatile temper."

"I'll get back up on the way," Phil says.

As DK gets out of the jeep in front of the apartment building, Pat and Phil get out, too.

"We'll wait outside the door of his apartment. Don't ignore that woman's warning, DK," Pat says.

"Trust me, I won't. He has already murdered two people."

DK knocks on the door, then stands back as Pat and Phil stand off to the side, out of sight.

The door is pulled open, and DK sees a very obese man standing in the doorway.

"Yeah, what the hell do you want?"

"I talked with one of your girls, and she told me where I could find you."

"She'd better have a damn good reason for running her mouth. I'm a busy man. So, again, what the hell do you want?"

"I would like to come in and talk to you about hiring some young girls."

Earl stepped back, opened the door wider, and motioned for DK to enter.

As soon as DK was inside, he flipped Earl around and cuffed him.

"You're under arrest for two counts of first-degree murder."

"What the hell are you talkin' bout? I never murdered anyone. I'm a businessman. I don't have to resort to murder."

"Shut the hell up while I tell you what you can and can't do. After that, you can continue to shut the hell up while I escort you downstairs and into a waiting police car."

When the door closed, Phil went back downstairs to await backup.

Within moments, two police cars pulled up in front of the apartment building to exit their vehicles and follow Phil inside.

***

Walking inside the house, Pat and DK laughed as two fury babies run up to them.

"I will pour us a cup of coffee. I am ready to relax in the front room and enjoy quiet time."

"I am ready to join you and toast another solved case."

CHAPTER EIGHTEEN

DK towels Pat's wet hair as she steps from the shower.

"A person could quickly get used to this treatment," she laughed.

"Any treatment you need to have done is only a request away, my love."

With a smile, Pat jumps up to wrap her long legs around DK's waist.

"I will take that as a request."

He places her feet in the tub and moves behind her as she braces her hands on the shower wall. Without a word, he enters her, smiling as he feels the warm moistness surrounding his rock-hard erection.

Her hips gyrate as he plunges forward, bringing a long, drawn-out moan from her throat. She feels his hot liquid shoot forward and a welcome pulsating rhythm pound within her tight vault.

"I think we both thought our request would last longer, but I must say, the ending was timed perfectly."

"I could not agree more, my beautiful wife," DK says, turning the shower on over their heads.

When they were both dressed, Pat walked into the kitchen to fill two glasses with ice.

"What is your thirst from the bar this night, my love?"

"Scotch straight up."

Sitting on the couch beside DK, Pat hands him his drink and sets her filled glass on the coffee table.

"Now, if my cell will stay quiet, this could be a good night for us both."

"I have no problem with that statement."

No sooner were the words said than the cell let it be known that help was again needed.

"Hello," Pat says into the phone.

"Hello," I am trying to reach Pat Lancaster, a male voice is heard to say.

"This is she. Can I help you?"

"Yes, my name is Detective Jeffrey Osborn. I am at the morgue observing an autopsy on a young man who was murdered some fifteen years ago."

"If he was murdered that many years ago, there can't be a lot left to autopsy."

At her words, DK's head snaps up to stare at her.

"The family had his body exhumed for the police to reopen the case."

"Okay, and now the question is, where do I fit into this fifteen-year-old mystery?"

"Phil Abbott told me you are a respected psychic, and I should get in touch with you."

"You have. Now, we are onto the next step."

"Would you be willing to come to the morgue and see what you can find out about what happened to this man? You were right in saying there can't be a whole lot left after this long."

"I suppose you want me to come now?"

"A body in the grave this long is not a pleasant sight or smell. So yes, it would be greatly appreciated if you could come now or at least within the hour."

"All right, we can be there in an hour or less."

Pat lays the cell down on the coffee table and picks up her drink to down the contents before setting the empty glass back down.

"I can already tell this does not bode well for our pleasant evening."

"Since you could hear some of the conversation, the thought of observing an autopsy is never pleasant."

"Why the hell is a psychic being asked to observe an autopsy?"

"A cold case is being reopened. The family has had the body of a loved one exhumed to try and solve the case."

"I hope I don't throw up. I'll come with you, but I have a weak stomach. I don't know if I can last."

"No problem. You can wait outside. I've been to autopsies before. While they are not easy to deal with, I can keep from getting sick."

***

DK sat down in a chair outside the room where the autopsy was being performed while Pat went inside.

"Hello, Pat. I am glad you are here."

"Hello, Detective Osborn."

He hands her a small bottle.

"Spray a bit of this up your nose. It will

alleviate some of the bad smell."

"Thanks. Anything that works is appreciated."

She squirts the spray up each nostril and sniffs.

"Okay, now we can get to the prime reason I asked you here."

He pulls a sheet from the mostly bones on the autopsy table.

Pat walks over closer to the table and looks down at the body, taking deep breaths to relax her mind and to try and quiet her turning stomach. She reaches out, touching a hand.

A young woman in her early forties with short brown hair and green eyes, dressed in a blue skirt and white top, stands in a well-decorated room.

A man who looked to be in his late fifties with black hair and brown eyes, tall and very slim, dressed in a costly black suit and tie, walks into the room to stand quietly, gazing at her.

"Sarah, why are you here? You were not invited, and I sure as hell do not want you here."

"I am well aware of what you want and don't want, Steven. Since I am not the young blond you visit at night to work off your manly needs, then creep home to me and the kids, I thought I would come and see the apartment you are laying out the money for her to live in."

Steven walks over to stand beside her.

"I have asked you many times for a divorce. I told you I would pay a hefty amount of child support and alimony. I want Cindy in my life. Why the hell, after seeing her, can't you understand this? I don't care what you want or what you think you need. She is going to have my child, so she for sure needs me now to be her husband."

"You rotten, egotistical prick! You only care about yourself. I can see that nothing I say is going to change your mind. I will wish you and your slut a good evening."

Sarah turns and walks to the door just as she sees the young woman who is causing her so much pain run into the room.

"Steven, have you told her our good news yet?"

Sarah steps back, looking at the young woman, laughing and staring at her.

"You are not the least bit sorry for wrecking a family? You only want Steven to leave his wife and children and hook up with you."

"Well, it is obvious I am the one he wants to spend his life with."

Sarah stays silent for a moment, gazing at the two watching her.

"I believe you are right. The two of you deserve each other. I will be going. Steven, have your attorney draw up the papers to have this sham of a marriage ended so you and your choice can get on with your lives."

Pat stepped back away from the table and opened her eyes.

"This is going to take longer than I thought. I will need the address where Steven had his mistress living. I am sure his family can find this information for you."

"All right, I will get right on that. Thank you, Pat."

***

Walking to their vehicle, DK had to ask what was most on his mind.

"What are we in for now? I know you did not solve the fifteen-year-old mystery. You would be smiling."

"You're right, I didn't. We are going to where the murdered man lived as soon as Osborn can get the address from the family and the okay from the people living there now."

"So, is the place we will be checking out a dump with rats running over our feet?"

"No. The place we will be going to is a real upscale apartment."

"That's a plus. Guess I can be a part of that without being an embarrassment."

***

Her ringing cell has her reaching into her jacket pocket.

"Hello, I take it we know where we are going to find out more about the fifteen-year-old mystery."

"Yeah, 1524 Celler Avenue, apartment 34."

"Okay. We will meet you there."

***

Pulling up in front of a very impressive apartment building, they both get out of the vehicle to walk to the front of the establishment.

"I sure hope they have good elevators. Walking up the stairs to the 34th apartment would be a little much."

"It would be a good exercise for both of us, DK."

"I can get all the good exercise I need with you." He smiled over at her.

Stepping out of the elevator, they made their way down the hall in search of the right apartment.

"Okay, here we go," DK said, tapping on the door.

A very handsome man in his early fifties with dark brown hair and brown eyes, dressed in black slacks and a long-sleeved black shirt, opened the door.

"I take it I am looking at the pair of psychic detectives Osborn told me about."

"You are partly right. Only one of us is a psychic. The other one of us is a police officer." Pat tells him, holding out her hand. "I am

Pat Lancaster, and this is my friend, Officer Walker. May we come in?"

"Right this way," he told her, stepping to the side. "I must say, this is a first."

"Things we haven't been involved in are what keeps life interesting," DK says.

He started to shut the door when it was pushed open to allow Detective Osborn to enter.

"All right, looks like we are all here, so I guess we can start. We needn't waste more time since I already informed you about this."

"As I just told these two," he nodded to where Pat and DK were standing, "this is a first."

"Pat, I hope, since this has been a mystery for many years, you can still find out what happened." Osborn sits on the couch beside DK and their host.

"What is your name?" Pat gazes at the man seated across from her as she relaxes in a velvet-covered dark blue chair.

"My name is Sean Matthews," he tells her, an admiring smile covering his face as he looks at her.

"I will need everyone to remain quiet and seated as I relax my mind to find out what may have happened here."

"What do you mean? It may have happened here. Don't you know if this is the place where the murder happened?"

"Detective Osborn, I never assume anything. Now, if you stay quiet, I will see what I am able to find out, and we can get out of this kind man's way and allow him to enjoy the rest of his day."

"Thank you, Pat," Sean grins with a flirtatious wink.

DK stretches his long legs out straight and forces himself to remain calm.

Her mind relaxed now. Pat sees the man she had seen in the room with the woman he had been talking to earlier about needing a divorce.

"I told you I would pay alimony and child support. I am no longer in love with you. It is time to bring our relationship to an end."

"You have gone out of your way to make a fool of me."

"I am sorry you see it that way, Sarah. Sometimes, things that are out of our control happen. This is one of those times. I fell in love with Cindy soon after she came to work in my office."

"You are not going to get away with this," she tells him.

"Since I am going to marry the woman I am in love with and who is going to have my child, I believe we can say I have already gotten away with this." He waves Sarah through the open door and laughs as she walks down the hall to enter an elevator.

"I don't agree," a middle-aged man

coming down the hall dressed in jeans and a black T-shirt tells him. "I think anyone as cold and uncaring as you does not deserve to live."

Three shots ring out, knocking Steven to the floor. The silencer on the gun keeps the blasts unheard by those near.

"Oh my God! What have you done, Pete?"

"What I was asked to do," he told her.

"But, who asked you to shoot Steven?"

"That isn't important. What matters is that you and your child can go on with your lives and not have to put up with the trash calling himself a man."

"No. I can't walk away from Steven. I am calling an ambulance. He may be a sorry excuse for a man, but he does not deserve this."

The man holding the gun reaches out and grabs her cell from her hand to throw it across the room.

"Whether you know it or not, I have done you a favor. Anyone who would leave his wife and kids for another woman and knock that woman up before she is his wife is no man."

"You and whoever hired you to do this are as evil as Steven. I am leaving." She turned to walk to the door.

"No one hired me to fix your problem. You may be a tramp, but you are still my sister. You have always gone out of your way to do whatever you want and screw everyone else. You are not going to embarrass the rest of the family."

Pat opens her eyes and gets to her feet.

"We can go now. I have found the killer, and he should not be too hard to find."

DK holds out his hand to Sean. "Thanks for allowing us to do what needed to be done."

"No problem," he says, reaching out to shake Osborn's hand before pulling Pat forward in a brief hug.

"I am glad you were able to find who was responsible for ending a man's life, Pat."

"Thank you, Sean. Now, we can let you enjoy the rest of your day."

Walking to the elevator, Osborn speaks up to let Pat know their next move.

"We can go to the station now. You can fill me in on all you were able to find out."

"I hope we can still find the killer. Fifteen years have passed. People tend to move out of state. Especially one who has committed murder."

"We'll find him. You know what he looks like."

"I not only know what he looks like, I also know who he is related to."

"Well, all right! Let's get to the station and get an all-points bulletin on the way."

***

"I was able to pull up the case on the

fifteen-year-old mystery. The woman who was having an affair with Steven is named Cindy Ashlin. Since she and Steven were never married, we can locate her address in the hospital records. Hopefully, she didn't habitually move around a lot."

"Since it was her brother who killed Steven, I hope she will give up his whereabouts to save her own ass from prison."

"She sounds very selfish, so my money is on her speaking up," DK says.

"And, too, since we want to try and locate him now, I will wait on putting out the APB. I sure do not want to warn him we're coming."

"I think we can leave this in your capable hands, Detective Osborn. If you need me, though, you have my number."

***

Seated comfortably in the front room, enjoying a drink from the bar, Pat smiled over at DK.

"I have a feeling this case will be solved quickly."

"I hope you're right. I am sure the family wants to replant old Steven as fast as possible."

Pat shakes her head and reaches out to pick up her ringing cell.

"Hello, Detective Osborn. I hope you are calling to relate some good news on the case."

"I sure am. We were able to find Cindy Ashlin, and with minimal persuasion, she gave up her brother. I hate to tell you this, but her brother died a little over two years ago. We checked where he was buried to ensure she was not feeding us a line of BS."

That is all good news. I guess we can consider this case closed."

"You can pick up your check at the station when ready."

"Have a good evening, Detective, and I will see you soon."

CHAPTER NINETEEN

"I don't know about you, my love, but I am ready to call it a night."

"I can't believe I am saying this, as it is only a little after 10 pm. I am ready to hop between the sheets, too. I will even forego a shower since we have not done anything to need one."

"This week has been very trying. I believe the body pays the price when the mind is overworked."

"I do not doubt you are right. So, why don't we plan on getting out tomorrow with the babies, going to the park, and getting some food for a relaxing picnic?"

"DK, I think that is a great idea. You always amaze me with the great ideas you come up with."

"Thanks. However, every time we plan on doing this, the phone rings asking for help."

"I know, so we can be quiet about our plans and not tempt fate."

Without a word, DK pulls her to her feet and escorts them upstairs.

Pat walks into the bathroom to prepare for bed. Pulling her nightgown hanging from the peg above the door, she starts to pull it over her head and then reaches up to hang it back on the peg. After brushing her teeth, she walks out of the bathroom just as DK pulls the blankets back on her side of the bed.

"I won't be long, he says as he passes her on his way to the bathroom."

"I will say my evening prayers, and then I will be ready to join you in a relaxing night of slumber."

DK walks into the bathroom, closing the door on any further discussion.

***

A handsome man with black hair and green eyes, dressed in prison garb, stands before her. The man is very sad and keeps repeating the exact words.

"I was innocent. I couldn't say where I was, but, oh God in heaven, I was innocent."

He is in spirit, and for some reason, Pat feels she knows him, but she can't remember where she knows him from.

"You need to calm down and tell me what you are talking about so I can help you."

"No one can help me. It's been ten years, and I am still in prison for something I didn't do."

"What were you sent to prison for? Maybe if you can tell me this, I can help you."

"I was sent to prison for a murder I did not commit."

"You need to explain as best you can why

you were charged with a murder you say you are innocent of."

"I don't just say I am innocent! I am innocent."

"If you are not going to tell me how you became a suspect, I can't help you."

"All right," he takes a deep breath, "what do you want to know?"

"We can start with you telling me your name."

"My name is Ron Weathers."

"Alright, now tell me the name of the prison you were incarcerated in and the state."

"What the hell do you mean was? I am still in the damn prison."

"Ron, you need to know something. You are no longer alive. I am a psychic. This is why I can see and hear you."

"What the hell do you mean I am no longer alive? I can feel my body."

"Okay, I can see this is getting us nowhere. I will get out of bed and go downstairs, and I want you to come with me."

"Must be potty time," DK murmured as she left the bed.

"I wish. I have a spirit that needs help. I am going downstairs to talk with him."

"Do you want me to come with you? I don't mind."

"No, I'll be all right. Thank you for the offer, though."+

Pat sat down on the couch and wrapped her robe securely in place.

"All right, Ron, I want you to come forward. You will be safe and have nothing to worry about. We will talk and see what I can do to help you."

He emerged and stood looking at her.

"I still don't believe I am dead, but I don't understand how I escaped from the prison and how I am here with you."

"Please sit down in the chair there," she motions to the chair across from the couch, "the sooner we can find out why you came to me, the sooner we can find out what is going on."

"I don't want to be here with you. This all has to be a bad dream, and the sooner I can wake up, the better I will feel."

"Ron, sit down and talk with me."

Her tone of voice tells him she is getting out of patience with him.

"Okay. You don't have to get pissy."

"Now, you said you are innocent of murder. How did you get blamed for this murder?"

"Someone was killed beneath a town hall light. A few people told the police that the killer who ran looked a lot like me. The town is small, and I am known by most of those who live there."

"Okay, then what happened?"

"I wasn't home when the cops came to get me, but my neighbor, a man named Sam, came over later that morning and told me the police were knocking on my door around 10 p.m."

"Where were you at that time?"

"I don't care to tell you that. My business is just that, my business."

"Ron, if I am going to be able to help you, I need to know where you were when the police came to your house."

"You are wasting your time because I am not going to tell you where I was."

Pat reached out and took his hand.

"What are you doing? I don't want to hold hands with you."

"That is fine. I want to hold your hand for a moment to offer you some calming energy."

"If you feel you have to."

Pat saw a very lovely woman with dark brown hair and deep blue eyes pressed against Ron as he held her in his arms. They were both nude. As she watched, they lay down in the king-sized bed and began to make love.

"Who is the brown-haired woman you were making love with, Ron?"

"You perverted bitch! You were watching us make love?"

He jumped to his feet and began to fade.

"Ron! Do not leave. I believe I can help you if you give me a chance. Also, when I saw what was going on, I did not watch anymore."

He turned and once again sat down.

"This woman you were with, I take it, she is someone you should not have been with?"

"Alright, yes! Jeanine is the wife of my best friend, Rick. We didn't plan on falling in love with one another, but we did. I could not let Rick know I was with Jeanine, and she will never tell him about us."

"Are you telling me that instead of telling the police where you were, you allowed them to arrest you for murder?"

"Yes."

"And Jeanine would not tell the police that you were with her to give you a solid alibi?"

"She could never do that to Rick. He loves her and their children very much. If he knew about us, it would destroy him."

"So instead, you kept yours and Jeanine's secret and went to prison."

I went to prison, and soon after, I was hung. What did I just say? If I was hung, then this means I am dead. Oh my god, I don't believe this."

"Now, you say this was ten years ago? Ron, we no longer have the death penalty here. Could you give me your hand again? I will see how long ago this happened."

When he did as she asked, she felt herself

going back in time. Thirty years passed until she released his hand, bringing her back to the present.

"Jason, this all happened thirty years ago."

"That long, and I still feel so sad.

"Since this all happened so long ago, I am sure Jeanine is passed on, too. Why don't you let me help you cross over and be with her again? Would you like that?"

"You can do that? If you can, then yes, I want to be with her. Please help me to go home and be with her."

"I want you to look around until you see a bright light. I want you to walk into that light, Ron."

"Yes. I see it."

He steps forward, then stops. "Thank you."

"You are welcome, Ron."

As he disappears into the light, Pat gets to her feet to return to bed.

"I have this song running through my head. For some strange reason, it reminds me very much of Ron," she murmurs aloud. "Oh well, be that as it may. He is happy. He is, once again, with his best friend's wife."

Pat slides into bed beside DK and smiles as she feels his hand brush her face.

"Bout time you came back to where you belong."

"I had a bizarre encounter with a spirit."

"Do you want to tell me about it or wait and tell me over breakfast in the morning?"

"No, I'll wait. I am pretty wrung out on energy."

"Okay. I'll let you fill me in when we get up. Good night, my love."

"Good night."

Pat stretched her body out straight and,

taking a few deep breaths, fell into a deep slumber.

A very lovely young woman with dark brown hair and blue eyes stood dressed in a dark gown, looking at her.

"Need I ask who you are and why you are here, Jeanine?" Pat said.

"I am here to thank you for bringing Ron home to the light."

"Give me a moment, and we will go downstairs and talk."

Pat sat down on the couch, and, following the movements of Ron earlier, Jeanine emerged to sit in the chair.

"All right, now tell me what you want to share with me. I have a pretty good idea, but I will let you tell me why you are upset after all these years."

"I am still saddened by the fact that I kept quiet and let Ron die when I could have spoken up and let the judge know that Ron did not murder anyone and that he was with me when the murder occurred."

"Why did you remain quiet?"

"I couldn't let Rick, my husband and the father of my three children, know I was having an affair with his best friend."

"Instead, you let Jason pay for the affair with his life."

"Please don't judge me. There isn't anything you can say that I have not said to myself so many times."

"I'm not our Holy Father, Jeanine, so I have no right to judge you. I find it hard to fathom how you could allow Ron to take all the blame while you stood back and protected yourself."

"While I visited his grave late at night, I was finding it harder and harder to live with myself."

"I can understand why. I also find it hard to believe your husband had no clue about your and Ron's affair."

"My husband was a very trusting man, Pat. It would never enter his mind that the woman he loved and who was the mother of his children could ever do anything wrong. Especially cheat."

"Did Ron ever visit you in the late-night hours? Or did you ever have dreams of him?"

"Yes. I had many dreams of Ron. I think this is why I did what I did."

"What did you do? Go and confess your sin to a priest?"

"No. I am not of the Catholic faith. But even if I had been, I would not have tried to get forgiveness for something I did not deserve forgiveness for. Instead of trying to live with my unforgivable sin, I killed myself."

"Again, I am not God. What you did is on you."

"I am going to leave you now, Pat. I came to thank you for sending Ron home and for listening to me."

"You are welcome, Jeanine."

Pat gets up from the couch, and as she does, she sees Jeanine moments before emerging back into spirit, dressed in a long black veil.

"I am going to go back to bed, and with any luck, no one else needs to be heard this night. I still wish I could bring to mind the song that Jeanine and Ron remind me of. Oh well. I know country singers sing a lot of sad songs, but I doubt they have ever written one as sad as what Jeanine and Ron have gone through."

DK pulled the blankets back for Pat to get into bed.

"Thank you, Sweet one."

DK reached out and pulled her over beside him.

"I'll keep you near so no one can ask you to get up and listen to what they have to say."

"I think I have heard all I am going to listen to this night. The spirits who came to talk with me had an affair some years back, and I guess the man was accused of murder and hanged, and the married woman he was having an affair with was his best friend's wife. Instead of speaking up to say he was with her at the time of the murder, she remained quiet. I think it is strange that their being together reminds me of a song. But I can't recall the title. Oh well, good night, love. I am going to sleep."

DK tried to fall asleep, but the song Pat could not bring to mind was running through his head so strong he could all but see a woman standing at a grave, wearing a long black veil.

CHAPTER TWENTY

"I take it you were finally able to get some sleep last night," DK glanced at her as he poured them both coffee.

"Yes, and that song finally let up and let me relax my mind."

"Did you figure out yet what the song is?"

"No, and I don't want to try. I don't need to keep trying to figure out the title."

"If you would like to know, I can tell you the title and the singer."

"Oh yes, you are a lover of country music. I rarely listen to country. I am still into rock."

"Lefty Frizzell sings The Long Black Veil."

As the song began playing in her mind, she smiled.

"That's it. I have always liked that song, and I am still finding it odd that I could not remember the title or the singer."

"I hear the older one gets, the lapse in memory is more noticeable."

"Oh, like you never have a memory lapse."

She reaches out to smack him on the behind as he sets the coffee pot back on the burner.

"We still have not gotten away with the babies to enjoy a romp in the park."

"All we can do is try. I have my job, and I can't ignore what I am paid to do."

Right on time, her cell begins to ring, making her reach behind her to lift it from the counter.

"There goes this day down the hole. I'll

go see to the babies." He pushes back his chair and gets to his feet. "I'll feed them while you are finding out what our day is going to have us doing."

"Hello," Pat speaks into her cell.

"Hello to you, Pat Lancaster. My name is Chester Rollins, and I am looking for a genuine psychic. I was told by one of the detectives in the Shillow Police Department that you can fit that search."

"Yes, I am a psychic. What is going on that you would need me to talk with?"

"Seems that my wife of thirty-four years is a cheater. So I don't need to blow the bitch, and her playmate away; I need you to see if this is true."

"Were you told that I charge for my services?"

"I have no problem with you wanting money. The only problem I will have is if you turn out to be a fraud."

“Then I guess you will have no problem, as I am the real deal.”

“Can you meet me at Halstin Park at four o’clock this afternoon?”

“Yes, I can do this. Until then. Chester.”

Pat lays the cell on the table and gets to her feet.

DK is finishing filling the feed bowls with Stormy and Ash’s favorite food.

“What is on the agenda for today? Ghosts or murders?”

“Seems a man thinks his wife is cheating. He wants me to find out if this is true. He sounds like a real hot head, so I am glad you will be with me to calm him down if he starts to become unruly.”

“I can do this. When are we going to meet up with Mr. Hot Head?”

“He wants to meet at Halstin Park at four this afternoon.”

"That means we can still have a leisurely breakfast and spend some much-needed time with the furbabies."

"I don't know about you, but I am getting hungry, so let's get started on filling up on some French Toast and another pot of coffee?"

"You read my mind, my beautiful wife."

***

"I'm glad we decided to bring Storm and Ash along. After you're through with the one we are here to see, we can enjoy some time in the park."

"Speaking of the one we are here to see, that is most likely him sitting alone at the table."

"While you are seeing what you can find out, I will walk around nearby with the Storm and Ash."

"Hello. Are you Chester?"

"Yes," he holds out his hand.

"All right, I will sit down here and see what we can find out."

"As I said on the phone, her and I've been married thirty-four years. Never in my wildest dreams did I ever think she would turn out to be a slut. Guess we just never know what is what."

"For one thing, Chester, we don't know if what you suspect about your wife is true. How did you begin not to trust her, and what is her name?"

"Charlene started turning me down when I would want to have sex. She never acted this way before. Hell, most of the time, she would beat me to bed to get it on. Then, about a little over a month ago, she changed."

"In what way did she change? Did the two of you start fighting over her not wanting to have sex with you?"

"Yeah, the fact is, I would get so pissed off when she started turning me down, I had to force her to let me get it on with her. She would cry and bitch. She's my wife! It's my right to screw her."

"You need to calm down, Chester. I can't help you if you get out of control. I want to inform you that the man accompanying me is my husband, and he is also a police officer. So, let's keep a tight lid on your anger."

"Yeah, guess I do get out of control now and then."

"Now, do you have a picture of Charlene?"

Chester gets to his feet, pulls up the back of his blue T-shirt, and reaches into the back pocket of his black jeans to retrieve his wallet. He removes a picture and hands it over to Pat.

"She is a very pretty woman," Pat says before placing the picture down on the table. "I will need you to stay quiet while I see what I can."

Within minutes, she sees the woman in the picture with a very handsome young man.

Pat can tell the man is some years younger than Charlene. They are both laughing and enjoying a walk in the same park where she and Chester are currently.

"Well, what the hell! Are you seeing anything or not?"

The scene she had been seeing in her mind disappeared, and she turned to look at him.

"I made it quite clear that you have to stay quiet while I see what is going on. If you can't do as I say, then I will leave, and you can find someone else to help you. One thing I am seeing here, Chester, is that you have a very volatile temper. You may want to consider seeking help with managing your anger. Charlene is not safe in your presence."

"Why, you evil bitch! I am not the one who needs help! You pretend to see into people's lives and charge money for your scams!"

He drew back his open hand and then

screamed as Storm jumped, knocking him backward off the thick seating around the table.

Pat jumped to her feet as DK ran forward to pull Storm off the screaming man.

"I just let them off their leash to go potty. I am sure glad I did. That sick bastard was going to slap you."

"Yes, he was. I want him arrested. I am going to press charges for assault. Go ahead and cuff him, then hold him in place while I see if I can find out anything more about him."

When DK did as she asked, Pat reached out, putting a hand on Chester's shoulder.

In her mind's eye, she saw Chester slap and kick Charlene over and over as he called her dirty names and screamed out his hatred for her.

"Someday, you filthy bitch I am going to kill you. You remember this warning!"

"I'll call an officer to transport him to jail.

As you know, we will have to go to the station so that I can press charges."

When the patrol car pulled up with two police officers inside, DK pulled Chester toward the waiting vehicle.

Pat came forward to meet Dk as he moved towards her with Storm and Ash.

"Looks as though our time in the park with Storm and Ash was very productive."

"Not to mention safe," DK smiled at her.

"I guess I can chalk this one up to a freebie. I have to say, though, getting a person with as bad a temper as Chester into a health facility is well worth it."

" Yeah, he is too sick to stand trial. I don't know about you, but I am ready to go play with Storm and Ash."

As though they could understand what DK was saying, their tails began to wag, and they turned in circles with anticipation of playing in the park.

CHAPTER TWENTY-ONE

Seated together with their feet propped up on the ottoman, DK turns to Pat with a grin on his handsome face.

"When I saw old Chester draw back his open palm, I almost beat Storm in rushing to knock him off the seat."

"Chester is an irate man. He could very well carry out his threat to kill his wife."

"Good thing for her, Chester called you to prove him right in suspecting her of cheating."

"And in so doing, he allowed me to see how he treated his wife. And to hear the threat he made on her life."

The ringing of her cell had Pat moving forward to remove it from the coffee table.

"Hello."

"Yes, hello. My name is Rodger Adams. I am trying to reach Pat Lancaster."

"You are speaking with Pat Lancaster. How can I help you, Rodger?"

"I understand you are a psychic."

"This is true."

"Am I correct in assuming, then, that you believe ghosts and demons exist?"

"Yes."

"Would I be wasting my time and my money, as I am sure you charge for your talent, in hiring you to get rid of a ghost or a demon?"

"Listen, Rodger, I can tell by the tone of your voice that you are a nonbeliever in the paranormal. So, why don't you tell me where we can meet and talk about this?"

"If you are willing to come to my house, I will give you the address."

"What is your address?"

"My address is 7240 Kingston Road. I

live out in the country with my wife and two children."

"When would you like to meet?"

"Would this evening be too early to set up an appointment? Nothing happens until around 9 pm."

"That is fine. A police officer will be accompanying me."

"Why would you need to bring an officer of the law?"

"The police officer who will be with me is my husband. As a psychic, I assist various precincts in solving their most challenging cases. My husband is the officer hired to accompany me."

"I have no problem with an officer coming with you."

"Alright. Until then."

"I take it we have a job to do later on this evening," DK says.

"Yes, a man leads me to believe he is being haunted by a demon or a ghost or both."

"Can't wait to be part of this."

***

Pulling up in front of a lovely white house, Pat opens her car door to step onto the sidewalk.

"I guess we are about to greet the ghostly inhabitants of this well-maintained mansion."

"We never know what is just around the corner," Pat glances over at him as they make their way to the front door.

DK rings the doorbell, then steps back to wait.

The man pulling the door open appears to be in his late sixties, with a full head of gray hair and a gray beard, dressed in black slacks and a white, long-sleeved button-up shirt.

"Are you Rodger?"

"Yes. Please come in, Pat. Would you

and your husband like to have something to drink?"

"We would enjoy anything cold and non-alcoholic, thank you, " Pat tells him.

"Coming right up."

A chubby black woman in her late fifties, wearing a blue dress with a white apron, scurries from the room.

Rodger directs them to the living room and motions for them to be seated in chairs in front of the sofa.

DK and Pat accept tall glasses of iced tea as they are handed to them.

"Thank you," Pat tells her before setting her glass on the end table.

"All right. I am ready to hear what is going on in your home that you have asked me to investigate."

"First off, I need to know what you charge. I am not a millionaire."

"I charge a flat $100.00."

"All right, that is affordable."

"Is your wife home now? I would like to meet her and ask what she has seen."

"My wife and children are with my mother right now. I would prefer they not be present while you are trying to find out what is going on. I do not want them involved in the paranormal. Especially the children."

"How old are your children? And, have they said they have seen anything strange going on in the house?"

"My two boys are twelve and nine. I hate to admit this, but they kept trying to tell their mother and me that they have been seeing a young boy at night who would disappear when they tried to talk to him. I kept telling them it was all in their imagination or their dreams."

"When did you begin to see they were telling you the truth?"

When they began having screaming nightmares every night."

"Did you or your wife ever think about having a priest come and bless the house?"

"We aren't Catholic."

He held up his empty glass, motioning the lady who had served them earlier to replenish their drinks.

"How did you hear about me?"

"My nephew is in the police force. He told me how much good you have done for the different police precincts and suggested I give you a call."

"All right. I will need complete quiet while I see what I can find out."

She relaxes back in the chair and, breathing deeply, closes her eyes.

A tall, robe-covered specter steps forward. A face of pure evil stares out at her.

"Why are you here?" Pat says quietly in

her mind.

The being steps back, staring at her.

"I am a psychic. I have been asked to find out why you are here, haunting the people living in this house."

The voice of the entity enters her mind.

"You will leave here, or you will die."

"You are wrong. You will be the one to vacate these premises, or you will be thrown into hell."

The specter moves slowly towards her. Then jumps backward as two spirits dressed in white appear to stand by the chair where Pat is seated.

"You are evil and not as strong as God's Holy Spirits. You will leave here now and never return.

Instead of leaving, the specter moves forward and is quickly wrapped in gleaming white chains... Within moments, the White

Spirits and the specter disappear.

Pat opens her eyes and sits forward in the chair.

"The evil has been removed and taken to hell by God's holy spirits. Now I would like to speak with the child who is said to have been seen by your children.

"I can't help you with that, as neither my wife nor I has ever seen the child; only the children have seen him.

"I will need to be taken to the children's room. Since this is where the sightings have been, I will have a better chance of speaking to the child that is being seen."

Rodger gets to his feet and motions for her to follow him up the stairs to the bedrooms. Once inside a room with twin beds, he turns to leave.

"I'll be downstairs. I am sure your husband will be glad to join me outside for some fresh air."

"Yes, I am sure he will and enjoy a cigarette too."

As the door closed behind him, Pat sat down on one of the beds."All right, I know you are here, so come and talk with me so I can help you."

She sees a young boy, who appears to be ten years old, standing by the bed.

"Hello, young man. My name is Pat. Can you tell me your name?"

Instead of telling her his name, he burst into tears.

"I am here to try and help you. If you can't tell me your name, I won't be able to help you. I am not here to hurt you."

"The monster kept trying to hurt me and keep me from leaving our house."

"I made the monster leave. He can no longer hurt anyone anymore."

"How do I know you are telling me the

truth?"

"What is your name? If you do not tell me your name, then I will think you do not want my help in leaving here."

"My name is Jerry, and I do want your help so I can find my mama and daddy."

"All right, Jerry, now we can get you home where you belong."

"But this is my home."

"Not anymore. You said you want to find your mama and daddy. I can send you to where they are waiting for you. I want you to stay quiet for a moment while I send for your mama to come and take you home."

For a few moments, all remained quiet. Then, a woman with a bright smile covering her pretty face came forward with her arms open wide. Jerry rushed to her and threw his arms around her waist.

"Mama! I have been so frightened. Please don't leave me alone again."

"I won't leave you ever again. We're going home where we belong."

The woman turned and, smiling, thanked Pat for her help in being with her son.

Pat waved as the two walked into the Bright Light of home.

The demon and the child are both gone now. You and your family are now safe."

She accepted the check, Rodger held out to her, and she and DK walked out the door.

CHAPTER TWENTY-TWO

"I talked with Phil earlier.

"What did he have to say?"

"He wants to get hold of other precincts to let me help solve more cases. I guess here of late, a lot of murders and robberies are happening."

He doesn't think you have enough cases to solve already?"

"I guess not." She picked up her glass of juice from the coffee table to take a few sips.

"I will talk to him. I think we have a right to enjoy our life without having to find bodies and ghosts and demons."

"While I would never deny someone help, I have to agree I am getting a little tired of not having a life of our own." I

The sharp ring of her cell phone has them staring at one another with an angry look on both their faces.

Pat snatches up the ringing cell and, without bothering to calm the anger in her voice, pushes the button.

"Hello."

"Yeah, Pat, Phil here. Have I caught you at a bad time? You sound like something is not right."

"DK and I were just discussing your idea to get a hold of the other precincts to see if they need help in solving their cases. We are in agreement that we already do enough for the precincts."

"I can't argue with you there. But, when families want to know what happened to a loved one, and you can give us that answer to share with them, I can't turn them away."

"You've made your point, Phil."

Okay. Then, are you ready to find out

what happened?

"Go ahead."

"A sixteen-year- old girl is missing, her parents are frantic to find her."

"How long has she been missing?"

"Three days now. We have talked with her friends and all who know her, and they say they have no idea where she can be."

"Who is the head of the precinct and where is it located?"

Well, this is the rub. We are talking about a police precinct, a good 200 miles from you." I debated on even calling you."

Pat glances over at DK. He lifts his shoulders in response.

"I have no problem with going. She needs to be found, or at least her parents need to know what is going on with her," he tells her.

"No problem, we will drive there. You

will need to have something that belonged to her, such as a toothbrush or hairbrush with the hair still in the brush. We will need the parents' address. When do you want us to come there? I think the sooner we get on this, the sooner we can find out what happened to her."

"It is already 2 o'clock, so say 5 o'clock?

"That's fine."

Okay, the address is 437 Beacum Road. The detective in charge is Detective Jack Reina. I'll see you there."

Pat ends the call and stands up.

"I'll see to the babies, and then, if you don't mind, we can stop by a fast food place and pick up something to tide us over. I don't know about you, but I'm hungry. In case you haven't noticed, I'm still a growing boy." He laughs as he makes his way to the back door.

Pat smiles and murmurs aloud, "If you were any more of a man, I would not be able to keep up with you."

Pat chews her Subway sandwich and grins.

"I forgot how good these are."

"Yeah, I've always been a great lover of these. They are not only tasty but filling."

"I hope I'm not tempting fate by eating something before I see what may have happened to this young girl."

"I hope she is with a boyfriend and not ready to come home. She is in her late teens, so this could be possible."

"I hope she is with someone she chose to be with. However, not letting her parents know what is going on so they won't worry is reaching."

"Kids can scare the hell out of their parents. I made a point of keeping my parents informed about my whereabouts, so they would be aware of where I was, and if I was going to be away, they would be informed of my whereabouts."

Seeing the address off to the side of the street, DK turns into the driveway of a beautiful three- story blue house.

"Nice house. Speaks of money. It could be she has been kidnapped for ransom."

"You could be right."

"Only one way to find out." She opened the door on her side and stepped onto the cemented driveway.

They were met at the door by a tall man in his early forties, with black hair and green eyes, dressed in a pair of jeans and a sleeveless black T-shirt.

"Detective Reina told us to expect you. Please come in."

Sitting down on a blue sofa, Pat sees a woman, in her late thirties, with dark brown hair and blue eyes, dressed in a pair of black slacks and a white sleeveless top.

"Hello. My name is Pat Lancaster. Can I ask your name?"

"My name is Cindy. My husband says you are a psychic and you are going to help us find our daughter."

"Yes. I requested either a toothbrush or a hairbrush with the hair still intact. This will help me to get her energy."

"I laid a hairbrush there on the end table for you," Jack says.

All right, now I will need everyone to stay quiet while I see what I can find. Also, what is your daughter's name?"

"Our daughter's name is Sarah. Our beautiful, sweet Sarah," Cindy turns away sobbing.

Her husband reaches out, drawing her into his arms.

Pat picks up the hairbrush and closes her eyes. Within a few moments, a young girl with long dark brown hair, brown eyes, and dressed in a pair of blue jeans and a yellow short-sleeved pullover top comes into view. She is a very pretty girl, although a little overweight. Pat sees the girl sitting alone on a park bench sipping a soda. A man walks up to where she is sitting and asks if it's okay if he sits down on the bench. Sarah nods and smiles.

"Do you come to the park often?" he asks. "I have never had the pleasure of seeing you here before."

"No, this is my first time here. I like to get out and be by myself."

"And now you have me interrupting your relaxing time."

"You're fine."

"What is your name if you don't mind my asking? "

"My name is Sarah."

"How old are you, Sarah?"

She looks at him, then replies. "I'm sixteen. How old are you?"

"He laughs outright. I guess I deserved

that. A man knows it is not nice to ask a lady her age."

"You never answered my question."

For a brief moment, an angry scowl crosses his face. Then he smiles. How old do I look?"

"I would say you look like you are in your seventies."

The angry scowl returns, and this time it stays, covering his face. He looks around the park and then reaches into his Jacket pocket, withdrawing a small pistol. He grabs her hand, pulling her to her feet, and pushes the gun against her side. "You will come with me and stay quiet. If you utter a sound, you will be shot."

Sarah tries to pull away from him, and he quickly puts an arm around her waist, pulling her close against his hip. They walk to a blue truck, and he puts her inside. "Don't even think about running. I can drop you within a minute."

He drives until they come to a log house in the woods. He turns off the truck and tells her to get out.

"You are nothing but filthy trash. Only a weak and ugly man has to kidnap a female." She surprises even herself as she laughs.

He stomps around the truck to unlock the passenger side door. When he throws the door open, he yanks her outside and throws her on the ground.

"I had plans for you, little girl, but since you said what you did, I have no more use for you. Without another word, he begins firing into her face until she is reduced to a bloody pulp.

"Too bad we weren't inside so you could look in the mirror and see how ugly you are."

With a hearty laugh, he gets back in the truck and drives away.

Pat looks to the back of the truck to see

the license plate, and then opens her eyes.

"I am sorry to have to tell you this, but your daughter has been murdered. I could see where she is, and I could see the killer, and I am glad to say I have the license plate number of his truck."

Sarah's parents began crying loudly.

I am going to get a hold of the police so we can find your daughter's body right away and so we can find and arrest her killer."

"Sara's father got to his feet and pulled out his wallet. "How much do I owe you? No amount is too much for all you have done for us in finding Sara's killer."

"I charge a hundred dollars."

He handed her the money and then reached out to draw her into his arms.

"Thank you."

"We'll be going now so I can alert the police."

Outside, Jack opened her car door.

"That son of a bitch needs to be found right away."

"Drive to the station so we can talk with Phil."

Within moments, they were on their way with Phil and two other officers to the place in the woods where they could see Sara's body lying on the ground, where her killer had left her.

"That poor child," Pat whispered, looking down at her body.

Phil walked up to stand beside her, holding his phone to his ear. When she saw a smile light up his face, she knew good news was on the way.

Phil turned off his phone and turned his smile on her. "They found the bastard. His truck was parked in front of the Busy Bee Bar."

"Looks like another mystery has been solved by my beautiful wife."

"Looks like it to me, too," Phil grinned at them.

With a wave of their hands, Pat and DK walk away to go home.

Seated on the couch in the living room, Pat takes the glass filled with ice and Scotch. "Thank you. This is just what I need."

"Yeah, me too." He sits down beside her.

"I felt bad about accepting the money from the murdered girl's father."

"I know, but this is how you are able to stay doing what you do. You do so much good for so many, but just like Phil and the rest of those on the force, you can't work for free."

"You always know what to say to keep me keeping on."

"You do the same for me. We are a good working team. Phil was able to see this."

"I am glad I was able to find Sarah's killer and bring him to justice."

"Trash like him needs to be off the street as soon as possible."

I agree, and now, Sarah's parents can lay her to rest and not have to spend their days wondering if they will ever find her."

"I would say this case turned out right for all involved."

"Here, here," she raised her glass in the air.

"I don't know about you, but I am ready to go outside and throw a few balls for our furbabies to catch."

Pat gets to her feet and grins. "Right behind you, my furbaby lovin' daddy."

CHAPTER TWENTY-THREE

Pat hurriedly opened the shower door to pick up her ringing phone.

"Hello."

"Hello, Pat. Phil here. Are you and Jack busy at the moment?"

"I was taking a shower. Jack is in the kitchen, turning on the coffee pot."

"I'll be brief then. We have a report of a missing woman. Her husband called in about her a few minutes ago. Guess she has been missing all night."

"Where was she supposed to be during the night?"

"He said she was with her daughter across town."

"I'm sure he has called the daughter to see what she has to say."

"The daughter said she was supposed to spend the night at her place since she was helping to take care of the newborn granddaughter. However, when she went to call her mom for breakfast, she was not in the guest room where she sleeps."

"Okay, well, let me get dressed and have a few cups of coffee, then Jack and I will come to the station."

Pat lays the phone down on the sink and begins drying off with the thick towel.

"I heard your phone ring. What's up?"

"It was Phil. A woman is missing, so I told him we would be at the station after a few cups of coffee."

"Why aren't we going to where she disappeared?"

"I don't know. I haven't had my coffee yet, so I am not thinking straight."

"Okay. I already have you a cup poured, so I'll go get the babies taken care of."

***

Pat rolled the window down to enjoy the warm air.

"Won't be too long before you won't be able to do that," DK laughed. "I saw the geese flying south earlier, and you know what that means."

"Cold weather is on the way."

"Tell you the truth, with the hot temps we've been suffering with all summer, I am ready for some cooler weather."

"You and me both."

DK turned into a parking spot in front of the police department.

"We're here. Hope this is not another sick-to-the-stomach case."

Pat glanced over at him. "Yeah, me too. I've had enough of those turnouts."

"Hello, you two," Janie said as they walked up to her desk. "I'll let Phil know you're here."

"Thanks, Janie," Pat said.

Phil motioned them into his office.

"I guess we could have gone on over to the daughter's house since you need to have something the woman has used."

"Yeah, we...never mind," DK looked over at him.

"Well, come on, I am anxious to get this over with as I have a date with my lovely wife later today."

"Sounds exciting. What's the occasion?" DK grinned.

"It's our 25th anniversary. Can't let that be ignored."

"Pat smiled as they walked out of the station.

As they pulled up in front of a one-story

brown house, they got out of the vehicle to follow Phil to the door.

The young woman who ushered them inside was very pretty and looked to be in her early twenties.

After they were seated in chairs in the neat living room, she asked if they would like a cup of coffee.

Phil thanked her and declined the coffee as Pat and DK shook their heads.

"What is your name?" Pat asked.

"My name is Kathy, and my mom's name is Trudy."

"How old is your mom, Kathy?"

"Mom just turned forty-three."

"Is your husband at home?"

"Justin is at work right now. He works at a furniture store."

"Now, did Lieutenant Abbot tell you I need something of your mother's that she uses often? A hairbrush with the hair still in the brush or a toothbrush."

"Yes. I have her hairbrush here on the end table."

Pat reached out, taking the brush in her hands.

"Now, I will need you to be silent so I can relax and see what we can find out here."

Pat sits back in the chair, takes several deep breaths, and closes her eyes.

She sees a tall, very attractive woman with short, auburn hair and dark green eyes sitting on a sofa, and talking on her cell phone. Pat listens to the conversation.

"How long am I going to have to wait? I am ready to have you here right now."

A deep male voice can be heard replying.

"You don't want me there by your side any more than I want to be there. However, you are going to have to wait until I get off work."

The woman laughs and responds in a teasing manner. "I can wait as long as it takes if the end of that wait brings you here."

"I haven't let you down yet, have I?"

"No, not so far. But I miss you when you aren't near, and that is your fault."

"I have to go. The boss is giving me mean looks."

"Okay, then I'll see you later this evening."

She turns off the cell and smiles.

Pat opens her eyes and looks around the room.

"Do you have a recent picture of your mother, Kathy?"

"Yes, let me get one for you."

As Kathy leaves the chair to get a photo, the crying of a small baby can be heard upstairs.

"Let me get my little one, then I will get

you the photo."

"No problem, take your time. I want to see your baby anyway."

Kathy zips up the stairs and comes back with a small baby in her arms.

"Can I hold the baby?"

"Yes, then I can look up a photo for you."

Pat holds the child in her arms and feels a loving feeling come over her.

DK watches her and smiles.

Kathy comes back and hands Pat a picture. Pat sees it is the woman she saw talking on her cell.

"Your mother is a very pretty woman."

"Yes. Men flock around her."

"Is she dating anyone now?"

"No, and I find that odd. Always before, she was going out almost every night, then suddenly her nightly outings stopped."

"Okay, I will let you take your precious one here, and I'll get back to what I came here to do."

Pat closed her eyes once more, breathing deeply.

She sees the same woman she had seen earlier, but this time she is not alone. A very handsome young man with black hair and brown eyes is holding her close in his arms as he covers her full mouth in a long, passionate kiss. The woman stands up to begin taking off her clothes.

"I hope you are not starting something you aren't man enough to finish," she whispers.

He stands up, pulls off his clothes, all the while laughing.

"You know better than that. I've never let you down before, why would this be any different?"

Not wanting to see the two having sex, Pat opens her eyes and sits forward.

"Your mother has been having an affair with a young man, who is quite a few years younger than she is. This doesn't tell us why she was not in her bed last night when she was here to help you care for your newborn, but a little more delving into what is going on will be needed."

A voice calls out, and Kathy laughs out loud.

"I think the mystery of my missing mom has been solved."

The woman walks into the living room and gives her daughter a big hug.

"What is going on?"

"When I went upstairs to call you to come eat, I saw you weren't in bed. I became frightened and called the police. I was afraid something had happened to you."

"You can't be serious. You wasted the police's time because I wasn't in bed? What is going on with you, Kathy?"

The woman flopped down on the couch.

"You need a mental check."

"Who needs a mental check? A male voice can be heard as he walks into the room. I hope you don't mean me. I'm fit and able."

"My mom is talking about me. I couldn't find her this morning. I was afraid something had happened to her, so I called the police."

"Are you serious? What the hell is wrong with you?"

"I was afraid. I just wanted to make sure my mom is safe. Lieutenant Abbot here," she nodded to Phil, "brought a psychic who works on helping the different precincts solve their most difficult cases."

"I hope you don't think I am going to pay someone for playing a scam on us. I am not that stupid. And I sure as hell don't waste my time."

"I always believe things happen for a reason. I believe I was summoned here to lay bare a secret that has been going on."

"Kathy, I am going to be going. I think I have heard more than I care to."

"You don't need to leave, Mom."

"No, you don't, because I believe Kathy needs to know what has been going on between her mom and her own husband. I've seen some real trash in my time, but woman, you take the cake."

"What the hell are you saying, you evil bitch?"

"The game's over, Justin. You and Kathy's mom have been having an affair."

"I'll kill you, you filthy bitch!" Justin yelled, lunging toward Pat.

DK quickly jumps from his chair and flips Justin around, and cuffs him.

Kathy stood in the room holding her newborn baby and staring at the two people who had gone out of their way to destroy her life.

"Kathy, while I know this will be a terrible thing to try and live with, one thing you need to know is this was not your fault. When those, such as your mom and your husband, have so little care for anyone but themselves, the only thing the people in their way can do is be glad they know the truth and go on with their lives."

"I want to thank you for bringing this to my attention. I will be getting a lawyer and getting started on divorce proceedings."

"Justin will be going to jail for trying to attack me, but you will need to get a restraining order to keep him away from you and your baby."

"How much do I owe you for all you have done?" Kathy asked.

"That will be taken care of by the Police Department," Phil speaks up.

Pat smiled and, as she felt DK's arm

encircle her waist, turned to follow him from the room.

"I'll meet you both at the station to pick up your check. And, Pat, you did a great job."

"Thank you, Phil. And we'll see you in a few minutes."

"Another case closed and closed well."

"Let's go. The sooner we get home, the better I will feel about all that has gone on here."

"Right behind you, my love. Right behind you."

CHAPTER TWENTY FOUR

Pat sits forward on the couch and picks up her cup of coffee.

"DK, do you ever wish you had met someone who is a more normal woman? A woman who can give you kids? I know you say you don't want kids, but I still think you could change your mind someday."

He sits down in a chair across from the couch and sets his cup of coffee on the end table.

"I hope we aren't going to start all this over again. You are a psychic, and I am a cop who, thanks to Phil, works with you."

"I know, but sometimes I get to thinking your life could be a lot more peaceful if you were married to someone else."

"What are you saying that you want a divorce?"

Pat laughs. "No."

"Good because I sure as hell don't want a divorce either."

Storm and Ash come over to lay their head on DK's knee to look up at him.

"I think they are saying they don't want us to part ways either."

"I think what brought this to mind is that mom having an affair with her daughter's husband. It is so hard to fathom the depth of evil in some people."

"Yeah, that shook me, too. However, getting back to your concerns about our relationship, and whether I ever regret having you as my wife, you can put your mind at ease. You are the woman I love and the woman I always will love. And you need to know that if you bring this ridiculous wondering up again, I am going to turn you over my knee and bust your pretty ass."

"Okay. Discussion over. We are well-suited and have two much- loved furbabies, so we will stay together."

Pat turns as her cell begins to ring.

"Hello, Phil. What is up this beautiful Saturday morning that needs my looking into?"

"We got a bad one. An entire family has been murdered. A man, his wife, and five kids ranging in ages from five years old to seventeen years old."

"When and where did this happen?"

"It happened about forty miles from here. It happened two days ago. Don't bother asking why we are just hearing about it, because I am asking the same thing."

"Who informed you about the murders?"

"The father of the man who was killed said he had been trying to reach his son about a hunting trip they had planned, and was unable to reach him, so he went over to the son's house and let himself in with his key and found them all laying on the front room floor shot in the head."

"When do you want to meet?"

"As soon as it is convenient for you and DK to meet me at the house."

"We don't have anything planned, so I guess you can give me the address and we'll see you there."

1428 Ashway Ave. You can meet me at the station, and we'll proceed from there. I already contacted the coroner. I am bringing about four deputies with me. I guess we'll see you in about 45 minutes?"

"Yes, that will be fine."

She turns off the cell and gets to her feet.

"Phil wants us to meet him and his deputies and the coroner to see what I can find out about the murders of an entire family.

We'll need to get ready to go. Please let Storm and Ash out for a few minutes since you are already dressed."

"Speaking of sickos, I think this will be another one to top the charts.

***

Seeing two police cars and Phil's vehicle, DK parks his truck across the street.

Even though I am hungry, it is probably a good thing we are empty bellied on this one."

Pat nods as she gets out of the truck.

Phil makes his way over to them.

"I am not looking forward to this one. It had to take one sick son-of-a-bitch to kill an entire family."

"I have to agree," DK walks up to him.

Along with the deputies, they make their way up to the front door.

"I hope the dad left the door unlocked," Phil said as he reached out to open the front door. As the door swung open, he walked inside.

The bodies were lying face up on the living room carpet. They could see blood soaking into the carpet and covering the walls.

"There's a good bit of blood spatter. If we're lucky, we will find some empty cartridges on the floor."

The deputies pulled on gloves and, being careful not to step in the blood, moved around the room.

"Rather than having to touch one of the bodies, I will look in the bathroom for a brush."

"Thanks, Phil. I would appreciate that."

Phil was back within moments, however. Instead of walking back to Pat and DK, he walked to the front door and stepped out onto the porch.

DK hastened to walk out beside him.

"What's wrong?"

"There are two animals, a small dog and a kitten, with their stomachs ripped open. This place is filled with so much blood and evil, I want to throw up."

"Yeah, I hear you. Did you see a brush or something Pat can use to tune into the energy of one of the victims?"

"No. I just had to get the hell away from all the blood and filth."

"DK patted him on the shoulder before turning away to go back inside.

"I'll go see what I can find."

Without waiting for DK to bring something for her to hold, Pat bent forward to take the woman's hand in hers. She sees a family seated in the room watching a movie. They hear a knock at the door, and the man gets to his feet to answer it. A young man is standing on the porch and proceeds to step forward.

The man doesn't allow him room to step

inside.

"Can I help you?"

"Yeah, you can help me. You can get the hell out of my way so I can come inside."

"Who are you and what do you want? If you can't tell me who you are and what you want, you need to get the hell out of here."

***

"Ask Delbert who I am and what I want. He can fill you in real easy." The young man has a smirk on his face.

"Delbert, you need to come here," he calls out to his eldest son.

Within moments, a male about the same age as the one standing at the door comes forward.

"What?"

When he sees the one standing at the door, he looks at him and shakes his head.

"I told you, Johnson, I would get back to

you tomorrow. I don't have the money you want until I get a chance to go to the bank."

"I need my money now. You have been stonewalling me for over a week now, and it is coming to a stop. I get my money right now, or all your family is going to be on their way to hell."

"Why, you ignorant little bastard! You will not be talking to my son that way. Now get the hell out of here before I call the police to help you get the hell out of here."

The one standing in front of them reaches into his jacket pocket and pulls out a gun. Before Delbert or his father can move, they are both shot and fall backwards onto the floor. Loud screams can be heard as the one brandishing the gun moves into the room and begins shooting at everyone there.

"You thought you were better than me, Delbert, my drug-addled friend. Well, I am here to prove you and your entire family wrong."

He begins pulling Delbert's family members one at a time from the couch and shoves them on the floor. Then he bends down to roll them on their backs.

"I want all of you to be looking your best and know that Delbert is the cause of all you losing your lives today. A small dog followed by a long-haired cat came up to those lying on the floor.

"Well, I guess I am not through here yet."

He kicks the cat across the floor and then reaches out to grab the dog by the neck.

"Not wanting to see any more, Pat opens her eyes.

"A drug dealer named Johnson is the one who did the killings. Delbert, the oldest son, owed him money. Johnson was no longer willing to wait. I am sure, evil as that sicko is, he will have a record. I'll come to the station and start looking at photos."

"That will be a great help, Pat. As always,

you do a great job.

"Yeah, the sooner we get on to finding that son of a bitch, the sooner he can be taken off the street, and people can be safe," DK delivered.

Pat placed her arm around DK's waist and walked with him out the door.

CHAPTER TWENTY FIVE

Pat walks outside to watch DK play with Storm and Ash.

DK laughs. "They like to start the day with a good ball tossing game. They know I can never refuse those looks of we're ready."

"They are both spoiled. They know we love them so much we can't deny them anything."

DK walks over to sit down in one of the patio chairs.

"You look down. What's up?"

"I don't know about you, but I am ready for a vacation. I know that every time we try to get away, the phone rings and we have to jump into another case."

"I feel the same way. I am so tired of seeing

blood and murdered bodies and hearing the crying of the bereaved family, I could yell. I would have said scream, but I'm not a female, so I'll go with yell."

"I know we have talked with Phil about trying to find another psychic to fill in so I can get away for a much-needed break; however, he doesn't want anyone but me working with the different precincts."

"He needs to understand it isn't a request. I'll talk to him and let him know you need a break. Maybe if he thinks you either get a break from all this or you aren't going to be working with the precincts, he just might change his tune."

"I have said it hundreds of times that it isn't that I don't care about helping find those who need to be found or those who need to be caught, it's that for a while, enough is enough."

"You are going to get your break. We both are, and then we are going to pack up Storm and Ash and get out of here for a while.

I'll talk with Phil, and while I do that, you need to decide where you want to go for a couple of weeks. Or even longer if that is needed."

"I want to buy a nice camper and go to the hills. I don't want anyone around for miles except us."

"I think that is the perfect choice. I'll call Phil right now, and we can get this plan started. Just one more thing. Do you have any idea who would be a good psychic for Phil and the others to work with?"

"Let me see if I can relax and try to find one. I know I can't be the only real psychic in this town."

DK pushed back his chair and got to his feet as Pat relaxed her mind to try and find someone capable of helping the police and others in their need. Minutes passed, but still she waited. Finally, she opened her eyes, knowing the quest she was trying to bring forth was a waste of her time.

Seeing her eyes open once more, DK walked the rest of the way into the room.

"I take it you're not having any luck in finding a psychic for Phil to call on."

"I am not finding a psychic at all. Why can't I find someone? I know I can't be the only one in this entire town who is a psychic."

"Pat, could it be that you are too tired and just ready to call it quits? You have been helping Phil and the police nonstop. Why don't you put finding another psychic aside for now? Then, when you feel like you are more in control, you can try again."

"I have no choice. I can't bring anyone to mind, and I am beginning to get a throbbing headache."

"Here," DK moves a footstool over in front of where Pat is sitting on the couch, "stretch your legs out on here and try to relax. In the meantime, I'll go fix us a drink."

"Thank you, DK."

DK hands her a glass filled with ice and her favorite scotch drink. She takes a sip and sets the glass down on the end table.

"Did you talk with Phil?"

"No. He wasn't in his office. His secretary said she would have him call me when he gets back to the station."

"I know he will try to talk me out of leaving for a while. Where I am right now, he will be wasting his breath."

"I agree. Right now, I want you to relax and not think of anything but our vacation in the hills."

"I hear the calm and acceptance in your voice. Believe it or not, that makes me start to relax."

"Do you ever stop and think about how much better our lives have become since we met? I do. There are times I wake up in the morning and feel this really happy feeling rush over me. I look over at you, and just the sight of you still sleeping beside me lets me know the happy feeling I am enjoying is thanks to you."

"Believe it or not, my handsome husband, yes, I do."

At the loud ringing of his cell, he reaches to pull it loose from the leather holder on his hip.

"I am sure we can guess who this is. Yeah, it's Phil. Hello, Phil. Thanks for returning my call."

"Vera said you called. What's up?"

"Pat and I are planning to get away for a few weeks or maybe even longer. She has had enough of seeing dead bodies and the like. To be honest, so have I. She is trying to find a new psychic to work with you and the other precincts."

"I know we have talked about this before. I thought she was determined to help when she is needed."

"Phil, what Pat does and doesn't do is up to her. Would you want to see dead bodies? Smell the rotting stench of blood and decay day in and day out?"

"Well…no..but this is her job."

"Says you. We are going away for a while. You can get busy solving your cases on your own. Pat is trying to find another psychic; however, until she does, you're on your own."

"I hope this doesn't end our friendship, DK."

"The only way it will end our friendship is if you give Pat a hard time about leaving to get some much-needed rest."

"No, I think too much of both of you to interfere in your lives.

"I'm glad to hear you say that, Phil. As I said, Pat is going to try to find a new psychic to work with you, but until she does, I would appreciate it if you don't call for her to help you with another case. Also, we would appreciate your letting the other precincts know this also."

"All right, you can trust me to do this."

"Take care, Phil. Goodbye."

"He didn't sound too happy. I can't blame him. My ability to get his cases solved and solved quickly adds to his being looked at as a very reliable Lieutenant in the department."

"This is true. However, he needs to stop and see the real successful person in all this. That person is you, not Phil. If he has any feelings at all for you, then he needs to accept this vacation you are going on as something that is much needed."

"We both know Phil is a good man. He will realize this is not his choice to make."

"I don't know about you, my beautiful wife, but I am a hungry man. What say we head out to a fine restaurant and enjoy a great meal?"

"Let me go run a comb through my hair

and get my shoes on, then I am ready to go."

"Good. I'll go start the Jeep."

Pat starts upstairs to get ready when her cell begins to ring.

"I knew this was not going to stop right away."

She turns on the stairs and goes back down to the front room.

"Hello. Yes, this is Pat. What is it you need?"

DK comes back inside, and when he sees her on the phone, he shakes his head.

"I am not trying to be rude, but I am very busy at this time. What you will need to do is call Lieutenant Abbott. He should be able to help you. Have a good evening."

Without saying anything more, she lays her cell back down on the end table and walks back upstairs."

"Not to tempt fate, but I think she is on

to getting herself into a relaxing mode," he murmurs aloud.

Seated beside DK as he backs the Jeep out of the driveway, she glances over at him.

"I am not going to feel bad about not asking what that call was all about. The person calling can do as I suggested and call Phil. I owe it to both of us to think about my health before I go down with a heart attack or a stroke."

"I am so glad to hear you say this. We have a great relationship. I don't want anything to change that."

"I don't either. So, now the only question uppermost in my mind is where are we going to relax and have dinner?"

"How about that new Mexican Restaurant in town? I could go for some good tocos. How does that sound to you?"

"Sounds like a winner to me. As long as they have some really mild sauce to put on those tocos, I am all for it."

Seated together in the very neat restaurant with the smells of great food being prepared, they talked and laughed.

"I can't stop laughing and enjoying myself. We have been out to dinner many times, but somehow right now it is so enjoyable it all but takes my breath away."

"You know you are entering into a new way of life, my love. A life that will make you more healthy and accepting of each new day."

"You should have gone to school to be a psychiatrist instead of an officer of the law."

"I know you."

"If anybody does, it's you."

"All right, here comes our food. I am ready to dig in."

"The waitress hears what DK said. She gives him a warm smile as she sets their filled dishes on the table.

"I hope you will both enjoy your dinner. If there is anything else you need, I am here."

Pat looks over at him with a wide grin on her face.

"I think you have made a real impression on our waitress. She was all but ready to cart you off to a back room."

"Meow." He laughed then, picked up his fork. "Do I hear a protective comment?"

"I have never been jealous in my life. Someone appreciating my handsome husband tells me I have excellent taste."

"So do I, my love. So do I."

Later that night, Pat lay awake trying to decide if she was making the right choice in wanting to stop working with Phil and the other precincts. She breathed deep breaths in an attempt to relax her mind and body and fall asleep. A man she has never seen before comes into her mind. He is a very handsome man, tall and muscular, with dark brown hair and green eyes. She watches him as he walks across a well-furnished living room to sit down on a light green couch. He stretches his body out straight and leans his head on the back of the sofa. Pat feels herself beginning to relax, and within moments, she is asleep, forgetting the man in her vision.

***

"Good morning, Sunshine. I take it you were able to get a good and rested night's slumber."

Pat sits down at the kitchen table and pulls over the cup of coffee DK sets down in front of her.

"Something happened last night, and I am not sure what to make of it."

"By all means, share with me."

"I had a hard time going to sleep last night. I was still trying to decide if I was making the right choice about stopping my helping all the police departments. When I need to relax and clear my mind, I did what I always do. I took some deep breaths, and a man I have never seen before came into my mind. I watched him for a few moments, then to my surprise, I began to relax and the next thing I knew I was asleep."

"That does sound strange. The reason I find it strange is that you're not being in control of what is happening."

"Exactly. I have never had this happen before. Tell you the truth, it is freaking me out a little."

"The only thing I can think of is you are working so hard to find a psychic to help out Phil and the other police departments. Could the man you saw be the psychic you are looking for?"

"Oh my god. I never thought of that. You could be right."

"After breakfast, why don't you relax and try to find out?"

"I think that is a great idea. What would I do without you?"

"I hope you never have to find out."

Pat laughs. "That makes two of us.

"I want you to sit down at the table while I get you a cup of coffee with your favorite creamer, then I am going to fix us some French Toast. Sound good?"

"Sounds delicious; however, you do not need to wait on me."

"I do not have to do anything. I want to fix our breakfast. Now, sit back, drink your coffee, and enjoy the great smells that will be in the air in a few minutes. Oh yeah, I am going to add some crisp bacon to that meal too."

Pat looks over at him as he readies the skillet to start cooking.

The thoughts running through her mind make her smile. The idea of not having to include DK in the different cases with murdered victims, the pungent odors of blood, along with knowing how the person suffered at the hands of a sick killer before their life was ended, strengthened her decision to find another psychic to aid Phil and the other departments.

"Almost there. This feast is going to be a belly filler like no other."

"It sure does smell good. Maybe we can both get jobs at a nice restaurant as chefs now that we will no longer be making money from cleared cases."

"You let me worry about how we will live. Remember, I'm the man of the house."

"I know you are the man of the house, but I am not going to let you be the only one working to see that we survive."

"As I said, you let me worry about what is what. I already have a few ideas of where to look for a job."

Pat sat up straight in her chair as DK filled their plates and brought them to the table. Before sitting himself in the chair across from her, he set a bottle of syrup and a small plate of butter down on the table.

"Okay. Enjoy."

Pat laughed before pushing back her chair to stand up.

"I will dig right in as soon as I get us both a knife and fork."

"That would be a good idea," he laughed aloud. "A little hard to eat sweets without a knife and a fork."

***

Later, seated on the couch, Pat stretched her legs out straight and, after taking a few deep breaths, closed her eyes.

She saw the same man again. She watched him as he moved around a spacious room furnished with a dark brown couch and a dark brown recliner. A fireplace filled a part of the room. Family pictures hung on the walls. A small black Peke followed by a light brown

Peke ran into the room and jumped up on the couch. A very pretty long-haired white and silver cat was asleep and only moved slightly as the Pekes settled themselves.

Suddenly, Pat jumps as she hears her name called.

"Hello, Pat Lancaster. I have been waiting for you to get in touch with me."

"How do you know my name?"

"Phil Abbott said you are looking for a new psychic to help the different police departments solve their most difficult cases."

"Are you saying you are interested in taking the job?"

"I am."

"What is your name, and where can we meet?"

"My name is Paul Absten. We can meet right here at my home if you like. Or I can come to your home. It's up to you."

"My husband, DK, and I can come to your house. What is your address?"

"My address is 542 Linch Avenue, right here in town. When do you want to come over? I will be here all day."

"We can meet you in about a half hour."

"Sounds good. I look forward to meeting you and your husband."

"See you then."

"I will get ready and get the rug rats taken care of."

CHAPTER TWENTY-SIX

"I sure hope this is not going to be a waste of our time," Pat says.

"All we can do is give it a chance. You haven't been able to find a new psychic, or at least one Phil or the other precincs would accept."

"I doubt any of them will even give this psychic a chance. And do you know why I feel this way? They know I always close their cases for them."

"Pat, I hate to say this, but I think you are feeling this way because you still aren't sure you want to give up your job with the departments."

She rubs a hand across her eyes and leans her head back on the back of the seat.

"Maybe you're right. I just don't know. I guess we will see how I feel about this man's psychic abilities."

"I think you're right since we're here."

The house was not a mansion, but a two-story house with a very nice paint job and a freshly mowed lawn.

They both get out of the car and walk up to the front door.

DK taps on the door, then steps back as the door is opened. They both stand looking at the man Pat has described.

"Hello, Pat and DK."

He holds out a hand to DK.

"Hello, Paul."

DK shakes Paul's hand in a firm grip.

"Please come in."

They stepped into the house, glad to see a neat and tidy front room.

"I have some fresh coffee if either of you would like a cup."

"I'll have a cup with cream and sugar," Pat says.

"All right. In the meantime, you can be seated in the living room. I'll be right back with your coffee."

They both sat down on the couch. Pat reaches out to take the cup of coffee Paul is handing to her.

"I guess my first question is, how long have you been a psychic, Paul?"

"Like you, Pat, I have been a psychic all my life."

"All right. Now, have you ever worked a case with the police to find a killer or a child rapest?"

"No. My finding missing persons is mostly what I have used my abilities for."

"You said, mostly. What else have you

been involved in?"

"I helped a woman find who killed her son."

"How old was the son, and how did you go about finding his killer?"

"I use a hairbrush with the hair still attached to feed into a person's energy. The boy was seventeen and into drugs. I was able to find the house where he had overdosed."

"How much do you charge those you do a psychic reading for?"

"I don't charge. I help those who need help. I am not into taking money from people who are already in so much pain they can hardly speak."

"If you take a job with the police departments to help them solve their cases, they expect to pay you."

"Did you charge people who needed your help, and if so, how much did you charge?"

"Sometimes I used my abilities for free and at other times, I charged $100.00."

"When you charged people, didn't you feel guilty for making money from their pain?"

"Paul, I am not a rich person. I work for a living, and using my abilities is how I earn my living. How do you earn your living?"

"Unlike you, I am a rich person. When my parents died, they left me this house and a few million dollars."

"So, if you take the job of helping the police departments solve their cases, are you planning on working for free?"

"Yes. I don't need money."

Pat leans forward and holds out her hand.

"Give me your hand, Paul."

Paul does as she asks and takes her hand in his.

Pat feels an intense, clean energy and is glad to know Paul is a man she can trust and, more importantly, a man the police departments can trust.

Pat drops his hand and smiles.

"You are a very good man, Paul. A man I will be glad to tell Phil, I have found a psychic who can do the job they need done."

"Thank you, Pat. I appreciate your time."

"I'll call Phil and tell him, as of now, I no longer work for the different police departments. That a new psychic named Paul Abston is a man they can trust and call on."

DK gets to his feet and once more takes Paul's hand in a firm handshake.

"Nice meeting you, Paul. I am sure we will meet again."

"Nice meeting you, DK. And yes, I am sure we will meet again."

"I guess we will be going now. Have a good day."

"You have a good day, too, Pat."

As they walked down the driveway, Pat smiled over at DK.

"I am happy to say, I have no more worries about Phil and the other precincts being in good hands."

"Funny, but I feel we have just solved another case."

"I feel the same way, My Love. Let's go home to grab our babies, then head out to a park for them to play."

"Right behind you, Sweetheart. Right behind you."

Judith Ann McDowell is a novelist. When not working on a manuscript, Judith, along with her husband, like to travel to different cities, such as New Orleans, to talk with people about voodoo and to talk with those who have experienced firsthand true hauntings.

Judith is the mother of four grown sons, Guy, David, Rhett and Nick, and lives in the Pacific Northwest with her husband Darrell and their two Pekingese Chi and Tai and three cats, Isis, Lacy and Keefer.

Judith is at present working on her next novel.

Visit her website: https://judithamcdowell.wixsite.com/jamcdowell